ROMAN PETROV

LUNA MASON

Roman Petrov

By Luna Mason

AUTHOR'S NOTE

Roman is a dark, stand-alone, mafia romance novella.

It does contain content and situations that could be triggering to some readers. This book is explicit and has explicit sexual content, intended for readers 18+.

A full list of triggers can be found on my website: www.lunamasonauthor.com

PLAYLIST

- *I know (faded), Ex Habit*
- *Alkaline, Sleep Token*
- *Till Death Do Us Part. Rosenfeld*
- *On your knees, Ex Habit*
- *i've been gone, Ex Habit*
- *Like U, Rosenfeld*
- *Kool-Aid, Bring Me The Horizon*
- *Undress, Rosenfeld*

DEDICATION

Remember, we don't let men tell us what to do... unless it's in the bedroom, and they have a big enough dick for us to want to listen.

Only then will we bend over and ***take it like a good little slut.***

Roman will see to you now...

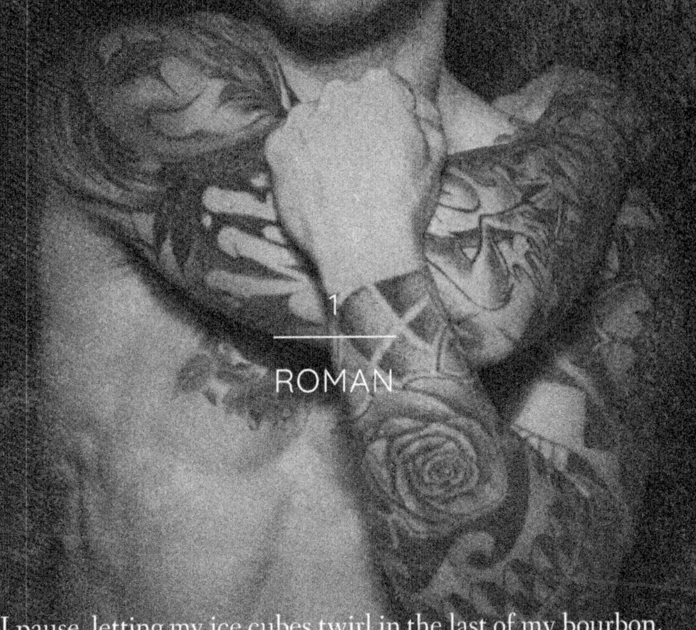

1

ROMAN

I pause, letting my ice cubes twirl in the last of my bourbon.

"I really don't think I'm going to make it, brother. The dynamic has changed and I have other things going on." Setting down my glass, it melds into the thin ring of water on the table.

He grumbles through the speaker.

I have half a mind to hang up on him.

"Roman. It's the ten year anniversary of Mom's death. Dad would want you there." Mikhail's words are heavy with a sigh.

"Our father doesn't give a crap. He's got that new pussy that's younger than all of us. That's all he's thinking about. Not that I blame him." I hope I can still get it up when I'm his age.

"Like any of us wouldn't do different? I can't remember the last time I kicked a woman out of bed."

Mikhail doesn't strike as the type to take just anyone into his.

"Yea, well, he doesn't want to remember Mom. He's probably forgotten all about her."

"Stop being a fucking brat, Roman. Be back in Chicago for Christmas. It's the least we can do for him." Anger sits just under the surface of his words and radiates through my cell.

"I'll send him a card. I have shit to do here."

"Seriously? Like what?" Mikhail doesn't try to hide the exasperation in his voice.

Sliding my laptop closer, I expand the image of the obituary on the screen. "Expansion, brother."

He snorts. "How many sex clubs does one man need?"

Zooming in, I find what I'm looking for. The next of kin listed near the end of the article.

"Just one more." Dragging up a new window, I click my cursor into the search bar.

"Well, whenever you're done chasing your dragon, the rest of your family would like to see you. I hope you change your mind about going home."

"Good talk, Mikhail." I end the call and slide my phone into my jacket pocket.

How was that name spelled? Ah, yes. Nadia Sanders.

Only survivor? It doesn't surprise me that salty prick father of hers never remarried. I've seen him at some of the functions.

I've nearly gutted him myself with how heavy handed he would get with the girls. Anyone who's run one of these places knows they don't make money if they're damaged.

This might be an excellent opportunity.

The blond haired beauty that glimmers on my screen certainly doesn't look to have the hard lines needed to take over in her family business. And she won't know how to maximize it.

One of the best parts of owning a sex club is the evidence you can acquire about the attendees. Everyone thinks that it's confidential and safe. But, I know how to squeeze every opportunity out of the debauchery that takes place within my walls.

I've used it to my advantage. There's not a job description that exists that doesn't have someone working in it that doesn't have deviant tastes.

I keep things above the law. But, I can't stop people from cheating on their spouses.

"Marco? Send me a statement on liquidable assets. I want to know just how much I can offer for a new location."

"Sure thing, boss. Might take a couple of days. The last shipment out of Chicago was delayed and is just now being inventoried." His thick accent is outweighed by his statement.

Seems some issues are hitting the home base.

Dad did say there were some problems, but he was getting them straightened out.

He is fierce when it comes to squashing out troublemakers. I learned from the best.

"Let's hurry that up. Throw some extra men on it. I want a solid offer by tomorrow." The faster I can take ownership of the Empire, the sooner I can start making it profitable.

"Yes, boss."

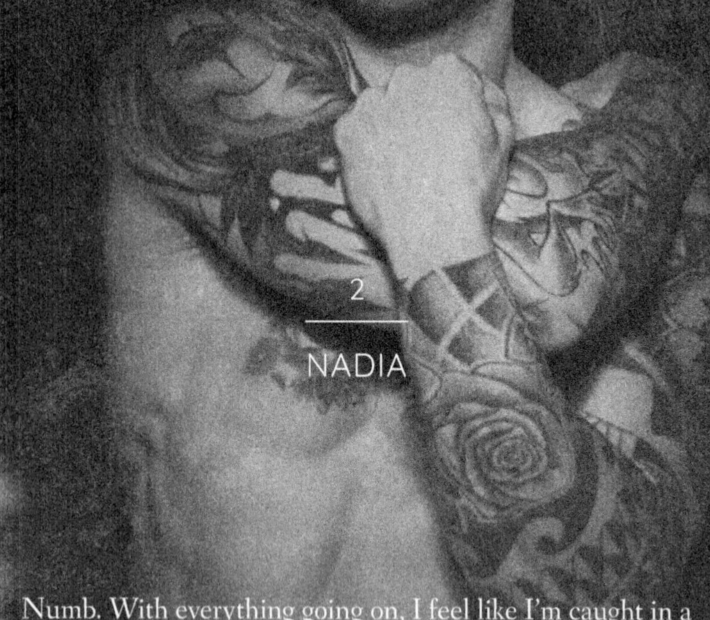

2

NADIA

Numb. With everything going on, I feel like I'm caught in a whirlwind of unknown faces, accounts, bills, and employees. And, they all want me to make a decision immediately.

I don't want to do any of it.

It had been almost seven years since the last time I even spoke to my father. He actually had the audacity to show up at my house on my twenty-fifth birthday and demand some of the money my mother had set into my trust.

Funny, he said he had "forgotten" when her funeral was, but he remembered exactly what day the funds were made available.

That was the only time I was grateful that my ex-husband was there. It was handy to be married to a lawyer.

"Ms. Sanders, the property in question is at seven-fifty Las Quatra Boulevard. I'll meet you there at three." Garland's voice has a slight nasal whine as he talks.

For being my father's attorney, he's actually been fairly cordial.

The building is just a huge, dark, rectangle. There's slits of windows on the second story, but none on the first.

It looks like a giant bomb shelter.

I know what he did in there, though. Why would anyone want to go into a sex club, much less own one?

A shiver runs down my spine at the thought of having to go inside. I've spent my entire life trying to avoid this place.

Maybe that's why I hurried to marry Carl. I ran off with the first man who offered to change my name.

Stupidly. Never marry someone who's self-centered and gone often.

I thought years of bad sex and emotional neglect was bad enough.

Getting a divorce from a man who knew the full legal system was a nightmare that I'm glad is over.

Garland's squat frame and slicked comb-over, hustles across the hot parking lot when he sees me pull in.

When I climb out of my Mercedes, my Gucci heels stick to the heated asphalt.

"We don't have to be long. There's only a few small formalities that go along with the will. You're the beneficiary of his bank accounts, and are also responsible for payroll." He shuffles as he walks next to my brisk pace.

"Fine. Whatever. Let's get this over with so I can sell this place and be done with it." I don't wait for him, but fling the heavy steel door open myself.

"Well, about that. There's some details in his paperwork you're going to need to be aware of." He doesn't look at me, but steps in front to lead me inside the building.

It smells faintly of bleach and lemons.

Not what I expected.

There are a handful of people milling around what looks to be a bar alcove on one side of the lobby.

They all very noticeably stop what they're doing and watch me walking in.

I bet they're waiting for their money.

Everyone always wants something from me.

"In here, please." Garland stands before a small office with a glass door embellished with a silhouetted couple vertically doing the sixty-nine.

Lovely.

Everything about this place is cringey.

"Let's hurry this along." It makes my skin crawl thinking about how many bodily fluids have likely been spewed around my father's space.

"Yes. Well, I needed you here today so that you can sign these paychecks and to meet the staff." Garland drops his briefcase on the huge oak desk and snaps it open.

"But, first, the will." With a flourish, he hands me the papers.

Reading in silence, I freeze when I hit the third page.

"Can you please tell me that this doesn't say what I think it does?" My smooth, glossy nails tap against the rigid page as I hold it up.

"I'm afraid you read it correctly. You cannot sell this establishment for ten years." He pushes his glasses up his wide nose and blinks rapidly.

"And, this part? I can't even give it away?" Why is my voice starting to sound more like a screeching hawk?

This can't be real.

He clears his throat and tugs on the sleeve of his jacket. It's like he doesn't want to answer me.

"That's correct. His stipulation was in the hopes that you would keep this business running." His eyes look gigantic through his lens as he watches me.

"No. Not going to happen. I'm not running *this place.*" My stomach twists and I can feel the blood drain out of my face.

Little stars pop within my vision.

"I need a moment." Dropping my forehead to my arm, I wave him out with a limp wrist.

This is too much.

I pull out my phone and find the contact named "BFF" near the top.

"Well. Is it sold?" Rochelle's croaky voice soothes the turmoil in my head.

"It's worse than I thought. Let me read you my favorite part." I fast forward through all of the legalese in the beginning and fill her in on my crisis.

"Can't you speak to Carl?" She finally says after a long pause.

"Why in the hell would I call my ex-husband?" Although, there are worse ideas.

"Because he's a lawyer. He can help you get this shit sold and get the money." Her exasperated tone shifts. "Girl, you have a fashion show coming up with *your* name as the header! Just think of how far that extra cash will skyrocket your brand!"

I roll the corner of the will between my fingers. My business is doing well on its own, but having the extra capital will really give it a significant bump.

"You heard what's in this thing. My father screwed me over. I can't sell this damn place. Not for another ten years."

She pauses. I can hear her take a deep breath before she talks again. "Maybe you should see about hiring a manager to run the place? It might bring in some extra cash."

I love how her brain works, always looking for another angle.

But, not this time.

"I don't want anything to do with this nasty thing. I'm not doing it." Anger surges through me.

My own father did this. Manipulated me into his debauchery.

I'd rather this vile business rots to the ground before I run it.

"Boy, he really messed this up, huh?" She breaks into a wild laugh that degrades into heavy coughing. "Let me know if there's anything I can do. In the meantime, Yolanda and Betty are doing their little primadona twirls, so I have to run. Love ya, chicka."

I know what I have to do.

Flinging open the door, I find Garland clear across the foyer. He's sitting at one of the high booths with two incredibly scantily clad women.

They need some damn clothes on.

"Bring me the checkbook. I'll give everyone their severance pay starting immediately." Waving my hand, I don't see if he follows before stomping back into the office.

Garland slinks in a moment later. "Ms. Sanders. I don't think that you—"

I hold up my shaking hand.

It's taking everything I have not to break down screaming. "Please. This is what I'm going to do. I don't see any other option that doesn't go against every fiber of my being."

His mouth thins, but he nods and pulls the ledger from the drawer of the desk.

After a very tense and stressful two hours, all of the employees have either received their money, or it's been stuffed in an envelope for mailing.

"Is there anything else you'd like me to do before we go?" His hand lands on the last of the lightswitches making darkness cover the windowless room.

"Yes. Put up a closed sign. Good day." Pushing back out

into the hot Vegas evening, it scalds my lungs, but purifies me from cloying ick that clinged to me while I was inside.

Even if deep down I know maybe I'm jealous people can be this sexually free without feeling like it's wrong.

That isn't me and never will be.

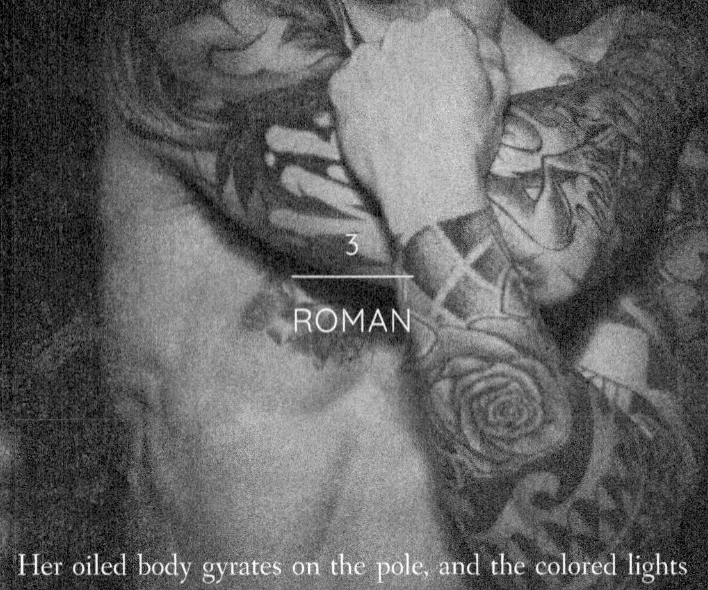

3

ROMAN

Her oiled body gyrates on the pole, and the colored lights are playing a rainbow on the small droplets that hug her skin.

She's gorgeous enough that I want to eat her.

If only she hadn't talked during her interview. Her voice is like sandpaper on a sunburn.

The deep thrumming beat of the song comes to an end and she lands in a wide split, dropping her bare breasts to her cupped hands.

"Nice job, honey. Now, before you say anything, put that mouth to work like those hips were moving." Leaning back in my chair, I unzip my pants and let my hard cock shift free of my boxers.

Her painted lips form into an "o" as she sits up. "Um, is that part of the interview?"

I let my fingers wrap around my hard girth and slowly stroke up and down. "Yep. Let's see how committed you'll be to your job."

Her nipples bounce when she sits back on her heels.

A ray of light cuts across the stage, then narrows.

Caz's heavy hand lands on my shoulder. "We got a problem out front, boss."

Shit.

The dancer's eyes widen as I stand. My jutting dick bounces before I tuck myself back into my pants. "Next time you can show me what you got. Talk to Marco, he'll get you scheduled."

She nods with a blank look before darting back to the dressing room.

"This couldn't have waited a few more minutes?" I'm stiff-legged walking next to Caz towards the main entrance.

"Sorry, boss. We got a crowd." He gestures at the milling faces that are standing near the double doors.

"What the hell is going on?" I ask Marco.

He's standing in the front, holding everyone back. "We're at capacity, boss. Some sort of fraternity convention this week staying in the casino behind us."

Well, it may be a good problem to have, but it pisses me off that I'll have to turn some of these potential customers away.

"How many can we take?" I start counting heads.

"Only fifteen more. There's over fifty. You know the inspector has it out for us. He'll be here in a heartbeat if we let 'em in." His graying mustache twitches as his nose wrinkles.

Yea. I don't like the inspector either.

"Fuck. Fine." I raise my hands into the air and yell loud enough they can all hear me. "I'm sorry gentlemen. There is only room for fifteen. You can choose amongst yourselves, or we can pick at random. Anyone who isn't chosen tonight, I will personally give a voucher for a discount tomorrow night."

After plenty of grumbles, the lucky ones cheer and head towards the bar.

When the rest file out, I turn to Marco. "We're going to the Empire tomorrow to see if we can make them an offer they can't refuse.

CLOSED?

Shit.

"We need to find the daughter." The sun beats down on me, baking me in my dark suit.

"How do you want me to do that?" Marco scratches his cheek where a day's worth of stubble has sprouted.

I throw up my hands and stomp back to the car. "Fucking Google, Marco. You're not older than my dad. He knows how to use a computer. Jesus."

He rubs his eyes. "Sorry, boss. I'm running on less than two hours of sleep after that college crowd."

Sighing, I slide behind the wheel of my Maserati. "Same. We need another location. If I owned this place, we could have bussed them over and made a fucking fortune."

The interior cools as we head back to the club, tempering my frustration with it.

If I can just find that Nadia woman, I'm confident I can get her to sell.

Her Empire is the key to expanding my own.

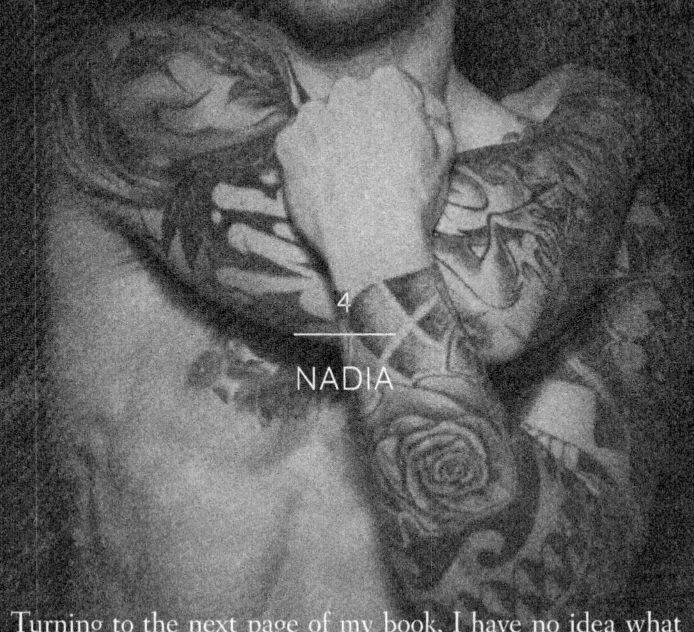

4

NADIA

Turning to the next page of my book, I have no idea what the time is anymore. I cannot stop reading. I have entered into a universe where none of my own bullshit resides. And damn, this is one saucy world.

It's not seedy like my dad's place. No, this is something else. Hence why it's fictional. The guy is a six foot five, wall of muscle NFL star with a huge dick that he knows exactly what to do with.

Maybe too much, the way he ties her up and fucks her into submission.

Every time he growls '*good girl*', my own cheeks heat.

During my marriage, I didn't have a sex drive. I thought I was broken. Now, the more I get lost in these fictional spicy worlds, the more I question my desires.

Not enough to ever act on them.

But surely there are men out there who won't just fuck me till they finish, roll over and start to snore?

That's all I was used to. Luckily, I'm an expert in finishing myself, especially with the help of my new toys. I don't need a man anymore.

I blink a few times at the latest line I am reading.

Wait...

Another guy has walked in while he has her tied up. My eyes flick over the words as quick as they can.

I squeeze my thighs together as the main character grabs the back of this guy's head and shoves his tongue down his throat.

Holy shit, that is hot. She's tied up and watching them.

I can't get through the page quick enough, the temperature in my living room is suddenly at a scorching level.

It'd be nice to have a toy, but I can't stop reading. Dammit, my hand will have to do.

I slide my fingers under my shorts and panties and am surprised how wet I am.

Just as he's about to shove his dick in the other guy, while that one is eating out his woman, there is a violent knock that makes me jump. The tablet goes flying and I tear my arm out of my underwear.

"Jesus Christ," I hiss.

My cheeks are on fire, my pussy is throbbing.

Whoever the hell is knocking has just edged me and I am not happy about it. Picking up my device from the floor, I set it down on the couch.

"I'll be back for you."

Because whoever this is can leave so I can finish myself off.

I fling open the door with a sigh and my breath catches in my throat. First I'm hit with a strong scent of his cologne and I scan my eyes up his body.

A navy suit, tailored to perfection, which means I can see how ripped he is under the jacket. He pushes his aviators to the top of his head of wavy dark hair and grins, leaning on the frame.

I wish I wasn't so horny right now, but I don't miss the veins on his hands and how I'm picturing him grabbing my neck.

I shake my head to compose myself, trying to ignore the wicked smirk on his lips.

"Can I help you?"

Shit. That came out harsher than I anticipated.

He pushes himself straight so he towers over me. I want to step back as he consumes my space, but I stay firm.

This is my house.

"Nadia, correct?" I can't miss the Russian accent as he says my name.

He extends his palm and I place mine in his. It looks tiny in comparison.

"Correct."

Sparks fly into my fingers and throughout my entire body, enough to have me snatching my hand back from his.

What the hell was that?

"I'd like to speak to you, it's important. About your late father's club."

Well, that is one way to kill my mood. A headache almost instantly forms at my temples.

Opening the door wider, I gesture for him to come in. I need a coffee and I want to hear what he has to say.

Maybe he can fix my problem.

He strides straight past, but stops in front of me, turning to face me.

"I'll follow behind you, this is your place after all."

My lips form an "O" as I look up at him, taking in that chiseled jawline, dark hair and dark eyes that smolder into mine.

Like the man in the book.

I bet this one could bend me over and pull my hair.

The power oozes off him, he could take control. Make me beg and scream.

What would it be like to orgasm from someone else?

I almost laugh to myself. This isn't a damn story. This is my life and I need this club gone.

"Sure." I step around him.

I wonder if he's looking at my ass.

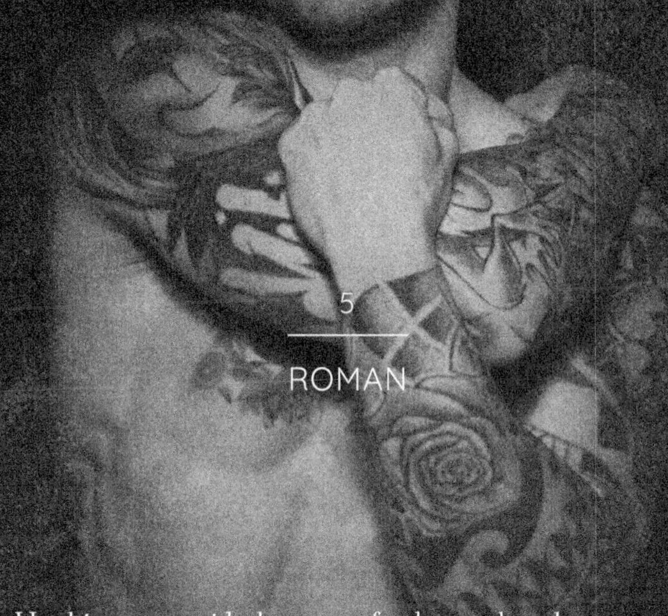

5

ROMAN

Her hips move with the grace of a dancer, but she seems to view me with a rigid stick up her ass.

If circumstances were different, I'd be tempted to try and break her.

The foyer is decorated in pinks, purples, and pastels.

"Didn't your husband get a say in the decorating?" Is that a flamingo vase?

"No." She doesn't slow down until she reaches the dining room and gestures towards one of the high backed wooden chairs.

She stiffly sits opposite me and folds her hands on the table.

"Where is he? He might want to be here for this." I don't see a wedding ring.

"None of your damn business." Her brow furrows and those full lips flatten into a scowl. "Now, say your piece."

"Your father owned the Empire Club." I lean back, crossing my ankle over my knee so I can watch her. "Are you planning on running it?"

Her back straightens and her cheeks flush. "Absolutely not."

That's a good sign.

Sliding a small card from my pocket, I flip it across the smooth oak surface. "On that is a number. That's what I'm offering for your dad's place."

Her chocolate colored eyes widen when she looks at it.

When that delicate mouth of hers opens and closes soundlessly, I know I have her.

"As you can see, it's twice the market value. I'll have my lawyer send over the paperwork this afternoon." I extend my palm in a silent bid for a handshake.

She just stares at it before giving the smallest of frowns.

"No." The tiny squeak almost sounds like a mouse chirp.

I couldn't have heard her correctly. "No?" My foot lands back on the marble floor. "You do realize who you're speaking to?

"Not a clue. Should I care?" Her chin twists like she just ate something sour. "It doesn't matter who you are, I can't sell."

"Roman Petrov."

The rosy shade on her cheeks fades to pale as she takes in what I said.

She knows. My name carries significant weight here.

I'm not to be messed with.

"Let me ask again, lastochka. I'm offering double the worth. So you're either stupid or—"

She holds up her slim hand, stopping me. "I can't sell, not that I won't. My father's will prohibits it. You think I look like I want to run one of those sleazy, disgusting places?"

What the hell did she just say to me?

A ball of heat forms in my guts.

"Clubs like that, and mine, are not the gathering place of the perverts of the world. It's where people can free themselves of their reservations and enjoy some of the best things that life has to offer." I'm tempted to show her my favorite thing that's hardening in my boxers.

"It's vile. Parading around screwing whoever. It normalizes cheating and destroys marriages." Her jaw and her fists clench in unison.

I've found a sore spot. What kind of person would I be if I didn't try to exploit it?

"Poor Nadia. You've never had a decent fuck have you? Is that why your dad's place scares you so much?" Once I verbalize the thought, I can't get the idea out of my head of throwing her across this table and making her scream my name.

She stands, shoving her chair hard enough that it rattles across the floor.

"You come into my house and speak to me like that? Get out." Her arm flings outwards, one pink manicured nail pointing towards the exit.

I like this fire in her. She's spunkier than my first impression.

"I know you haven't. Shame, I bet you're the perfect submissive deep down." I have no doubts. This prudish act is hiding that she's practically begging to be controlled.

Her little gasp makes my dick twitch.

"I bet you'd like it if I made you get on your knees and let me spank those pretty cheeks with my cock, wouldn't you?" I catch her brief glance at the growing bulge in my slacks.

"You'll never know, Mr Petrov." She crosses her arms across her belly and brushes past me to the entrance.

Opening the heavy door, my men shuffle to their feet where they've been waiting.

"We are quite done here. I want you to leave." Nadia looks up to the ceiling as I grow closer.

She knows I saw what she was looking at.

Leaning in, my lips dance a breath away from her ear. "Don't worry, I'll make sure you enjoy yourself."

Gesturing to my men, they follow me back to my car.

When I start the ignition, I see her standing on the front step with fire in her eyes.

There's no way in hell I'm going to let her win.

I'm going to get the Empire. Watching her shatter is going to make that victory even sweeter.

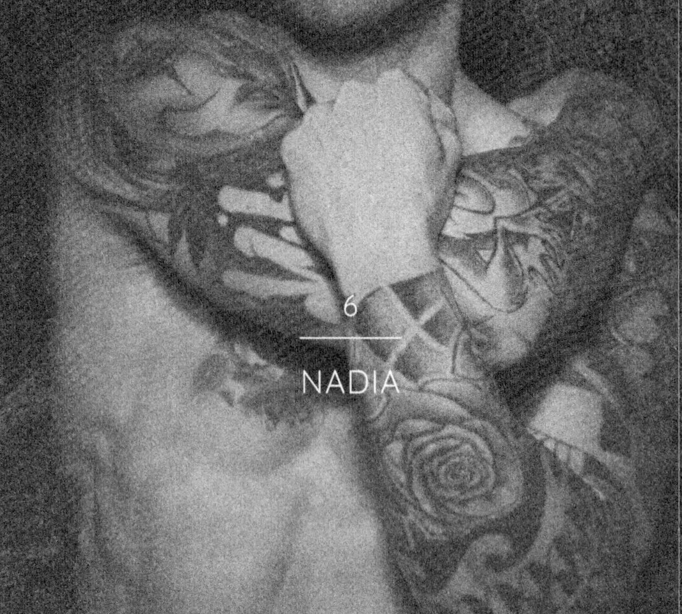

6

NADIA

"How much did you say it is?" Rochelle asks me for the third time.

Repeating myself doesn't make it any less. "Almost twelve grand. A month." Waving the paper in my hand, I wish for myself that I could blow off a zero or two.

"That's so crazy! I had no idea property taxes in Vegas were that high. And, you're stuck with it." Her voice has that high pitch she saves for stressful situations. Usually I only hear it at the fashion shows when it's our products walking the line.

"My only option would be to let it go in default. Except—" I take a deep breath. "—I already signed the acceptance paperwork before I realized. I'm liable." Tears threaten to spill over for the third time since getting the statement this morning from the city.

I'm so screwed.

Our clothing line has tapped both of our resources. We've invested every penny of liquid assets we own into promotion.

She's quiet a long time. "Well, I'm sure something will come up? Are you still going to be at the shop later?"

At least her tone has dropped back down into a less abrasive range.

"I've had two lawyers look into it. They both say there isn't much I can do except open a case before a judge. But, that could take months or even years because of back-log." I absolutely hate my father for putting me into this situation. I should have just hung up the phone when Garland reached out after my dad died.

"Well, I gotta get back on the sewing machine. I'll see you in a bit? Donuts from Maple's?"

Her sweet tooth will be the death of her.

But, she's hard to say "no" to.

"Sure. I'll be there soon." The tax paper is crumpled from me carrying it around, so I let it drift back to my desk.

If there was some way out of this, I'd sign it over to that Roman character for free if I knew how.

That man. His stare was unnerving. And, the things he said made me so angry, but so...something else. I'm not sure if I liked it or not.

It was hard not to think about him before I went to bed. His dark eyes and what they'd look like watching me from above.

Like one of the men in my books. Dominant. Powerful. And perhaps a little scary?

What commands would he give that I would relent and follow?

No. Shaking my head, I try to shove that asshole from my thoughts.

I have to work twice as hard now, and hope that when I can finally sell the club, I do more than break even.

Okay, keys, phone, designs, fabric sample bag, water

bottle. I think I have everything.

But, as I step out of my door, I nearly drop it all on the porch.

He's here.

My jaw sets itself as I scowl at him.

He's leaning against his car, all perfect looking smoking a cigarette. Like he's *supposed* to be there.

Whatever. I don't have the time or the patience for him.

Trying to ignore him, I'm painfully aware of him pushing away from the side of his Maserati and stamping out his smoke before he ambles closer. He slides a folder from under his elbow and steps into my space, blocking me from getting into my own vehicle.

The paper smacks softly as it lands on the roof of my Audi, yet he still hasn't said a word.

Arching my chin, I try to give the best impatient expression I can muster. "You're in my way."

Is he really leaning against *my* car like he owns it?

"I had a lawyer look into it. I have a new proposal that could solve both of our problems."

He gestures at the stapled document in front of me.

When I glance down at the large letters across the top, the heading makes my stomach roll.

"Marriage? How the hell does that fix anything?" Why would I ever put myself through that misery again?

"Simple. We tie the knot. Then after a couple of months, you add my name to the deed, like a married couple would. And, six months later, we divorce. I take the club, you take the cash."

He has a smug smile teasing his lips.

It almost makes him look handsome. If he wasn't such an ass.

I hate this. But, it's the first glimmer of escape I've seen.

"How much?"

His hands dive into the pockets of his designer pants and he rocks back on his heels. "My original offer stands."

"I want half up front." I need to get out of the burden of this debt.

One of his dark-suited arms snakes out to pin the papers and his lips whisper close to my ear. "So you'll marry me?"

Jerking my head away, all I can see is his mouth, inches from mine. "It's a paper marriage, don't get excited."

His body moves to mirror mine, but he doesn't touch me. "I don't think I'm the one that will have a problem controlling myself."

Roman drops to one knee, and holds his hand up expectantly. "I suppose I should do this the right way."

My cheeks burn and I frantically look around to see if anyone is watching. "Get up, you're embarrassing us both."

He chuckles, and stands slowly before patting the dirt from his pants. Opening my car, he takes my hand and leads me into the driver's side.

"I'll see you tomorrow, wife." He pulls the seat belt down across my chest and snaps it into the buckle. The heat of his breath burns my throat as he pauses with his eyes level to mine.

"Drive safe."

A vacuum sucks all the air from the car as he pulls away and shuts my door.

Holy shit. What was that?

Why is my stomach twisting into a knot?

What am I thinking? Marrying a man with his reputation is the wrong plan.

But, there's a piece of me that is curious what other tattoos cover his body.

Rochelle is going to freak out when I tell her.

7

ROMAN

SONG, TILL DEATH DO US PART,
ROSENFELD.

Tugging on the sleeve of my Armani pulls it down to just cover my diamond cufflinks. I haven't pulled these out for a while, not since one of the strippers tried to steal them a few months ago.

Without the cheese, there aren't as many mice.

"What happens if she backs out, boss?" Marco slides his sunglasses over his forehead to perch them on the top of his head.

This little chapel is dark compared to the Nevada sun scorching us outside.

"She won't. She had my favorite look in her eyes." I try to sound confident, but there's a touch of nerves in my stomach. Why? I have no idea.

"Huh. What look is that?" He stretches himself out on a neon pink pew and crosses his leg.

My phone vibrates in the pocket of my jacket. For a moment, I have a flash of fear that it might be her.

"Desperation." I answer without looking up from the screen.

Dad's serious photo is the background as he calls.

"Hi." I already know why he's calling. I need to make a mental note to smack Mikhail the next time I see him.

"Son. I heard today is a big day. I'm a little disappointed I wasn't invited." His deep familiar voice has a tinge of hurt behind his words.

"Don't be. This is just a business arrangement. I'll be sure to let you know whenever I do it for real." The anger at him for replacing Mom wars with my need to want to include him.

He's always put us first even after she died, and drove us to be the men we are.

Doesn't mean I can't be pissed at him for landing some girl younger than me.

But, it makes me want to be him when I'm his age.

"Well, be that as it may, congratulations, Roman. I hope you find happiness from this deal, then."

Can I find it? What would it be like to be with the same woman forever? To have her just be mine?

It makes my cock twitch.

No, that isn't for me. I'm made for the buffet. It's why I need more clubs, so I can have more dancers to do with as I please.

Although, having one that knows exactly what I want, does have its appeal.

"Thanks, dad. I appreciate the call. I'll get back to you tonight with the breakdown on the last shipment." Peeling back my sleeve, I check my Rolex.

She's almost five minutes late. And, she strikes me as the punctual type.

"Don't worry about it today. Enjoy your honeymoon. Well, with, or without, your bride." He's still chuckling as he hangs up.

The air moves as the door to the chapel is flung open.

Nadia rushes in, red faced and with a glisten of sweat along her forehead.

She almost looks freshly fucked.

Except she still walks like she has that stick up her ass.

One night with me, and I'd have her crawling.

Damn. The thought of having her on her knees makes me hard.

"Was starting to think you changed your mind." I give her my best charming smile.

Her lips flatten. "I did think about it. But, then the city called to tell me that my property taxes on that place are overdue." Her nostrils flare, but she maintains her composure. "So, let's get this over with. Did you bring my check?" Her hand flattens as her chocolate colored eyes look up at me expectantly.

I pull my wallet out and unfold the slip. "I'd like it if you begged a little harder."

There it is. That red blush works up her neck to accentuate her bright lips that purse as she watches me.

Fuck, I'd love to look into her eyes when I tighten my fingers around that slender neck and squeeze.

"Please?" she whispers.

I lay the payment across her palm and cover it with my own. "Good girl." Turning away, I readjust my crotch before rapping on the window to the office as she clears her throat next to me.

A grin twitches on my lips. If the praise got to her, I wonder what would happen if I made her my good little slut.

"It's time," I call through the shingled window.

The door opens, and the first thing I see is sparkly skin tight white pants with golden stars.

But, then I see his hair. A giant black skunk has died upon the head of a short, fat, greasy Elvis impersonator.

"Welcome very much." His lip snarl is on point.

Some days, I fucking hate Vegas.

"Let's get this over with," I growl at him.

"Wait." Her hand touches my arm and it races fire up into my chest. "It's my wedding, too." She turns to the squatty man. "I would like the full show."

Smiling, she steps away from me.

The short chaplain grins at me and follows her. "Why thank you, little lady."

My eyes hurt from rolling them as he hip waggles, stabs his finger into the air, and gyrates awkwardly through the short ceremony.

But, the smile on her face makes it tolerable.

It makes something inside of me warm watching her give in to laughter at his antics.

She sets aside every ounce of humor when he tells her to slide the ring on my finger.

Why does this feel so...real?

Her eyes lock on to me as we repeat back the vows.

I can't believe I just did this.

She's mine.

Tied to me more firmly than any piece of paper.

And for some damn reason, I don't want to let that go.

"You may now kiss your bride." His practiced words hit me with a force I didn't expect.

My hand wraps behind her neck, tugging her closer. Tipping her chin with my thumb, I go in with the plan of a quick peck.

But, her warm fingers trail to the base of my throat and fold into my collar. When my lips find hers, they're soft and inviting.

A shudder of electricity runs through me as I fall deeper into her tentative, but permissive kiss.

Hunger rushes through me and I give in, pushing my tongue between her teeth to consume her.

They clamp down, pinching me with a shock before I withdraw quickly.

Her narrow eyes tell me I overstepped.

I don't care. It was worth it.

"Well, I'm all shook up! I now pronounce you hubba hubba and wife!" The round minister claps his hands before heading back towards his office.

We both stand and stare at each other before she speaks.

"Only on paper, Mr. Petrov." She pivots and brushes past me.

"Oh, lastochka, the things I would do to you, you'd never want to leave." Reaching out, I manage to swat her on one of her firm ass cheeks before she's too far.

She jumps with a delicious gasp.

"Let's just sign the license and leave. I have work to do."

I put my signature next to hers, and then hold the door to the exit.

"I'll see you at home, dear." I wink and saunter to my car. "Marco, you're with me."

Marco's salt and pepper brows rise onto his forehead. "But, boss-I-uh. Nevermind." He jumps into the passenger seat.

"You're going to drive her car home."

"Um. Boss, she's in it. Right now." He points ahead of us where her tail lights flash before pulling into her driveway.

"I gotta take my wife home. She won't know where it is. You're gonna make sure her Audi gets delivered for her." I slide my Maserati beside her vehicle and slip the car into park.

"I don't get it, boss. You had me send the guys over to empty the place." Marco slumps back and pulls his sunglasses down.

"But, she doesn't know that. Go ahead and take hers. Here's the key." I hand him the copy I had made.

She has no idea she just signed a deal with the devil.

I can hear her squeal before she runs back outside.

Her face is puffy with anger as she stomps over to my window.

To her credit, she barely seems to notice that Marco is leaving in her ride.

"Where is my stuff? Why did he just take my car?" Her voice climbs with each question.

I slide out, and wrap my arm gently around her waist, then guide her around the front of the Maserati.

"Wife. I'm bringing you home. Now that you're married to me, you aren't safe here by yourself." I coax her in, and slide the belt over her lap, much like I did the other day after my "proposal".

She shakes her head with a vacant look. "No. This isn't what we agreed on."

"Yes it is." I rev the engine before backing out. "When you signed your name, you became my responsibility. I don't take that lightly."

"I don't think that's what that meant." Her lower lip sticks out.

I'm tempted to park and take that offending pout between my teeth.

"Well, I can take you back. If you die, I'll just get the club, and I'll get to keep the money." I slow down and pull to the side of the road.

"Um. I don't want that either." Her brows furrow as she stares straight out the windshield with her arms crossed over her chest.

"Then it's settled." I veer back out into traffic and hit the accelerator hard enough to force us back into our seats. "You're stuck with me."

"WHERE IS SHE?" My cook blinks rapidly when I ask her for the third time.

"I informed her it was dinner time. She said she wasn't hungry." Her gray hair is tucked neatly under a bonnet, but she nervously tugs on a stray strand.

Waving her away, I head up the stairs.

Nadia's door is closed.

I should have just made her sleep in my room. It would have opened her eyes to one of the massive, er, perks of being with a Petrov man.

My fist beats against the hollow wood. "Nadia! The least you can do is spend your honeymoon with your husband over a meal."

"No, thank you." Her voice is muffled.

"You'll not disrespect Mrs. Jenkins. She works hard every day to put good food on my table." My hand clenches to pound again.

The door flings open.

I can't stop my gaze from traveling down her scantily clad body. The tiny, low slung shorts hug the apex of her thighs. Her bare belly is taut beneath a short halter top that barely covers her full breasts pushing against the thin fabric.

My cock jerks when I spy her nipples poking through.

Jesus. She isn't wearing a bra.

"I already told her I appreciated what she did, and that I would find the leftovers in the fridge if I didn't make it down." Her dark eyes are narrow as she scowls at me.

All I can see is the low cut of her top hanging over her perky, tight—

"Hey!" Her palm shoves against my chest, knocking me backwards.

"What?" I'm having a hard time focusing on anything else but her body.

She follows in into the hall and snaps her fingers in front of my nose. "Whatever 'this' is." She waves her hand in front of my face. "It isn't happening. We are only married on paper."

Now, she's pissing me off.

Before I can stop myself, my grip wraps around her throat and pins her to the far wall.

Fuck, I can feel her squirm against me. She's making me want to take what is mine.

"I could make you scream, and not a soul in this building will come and stop me." My knee pushes between her thighs so she can get the full effect of just how ready I am.

The mint of her rapid breath tickles my neck. "You wouldn't dare."

Heat burns through my suit as my chest presses against hers.

"Oh, lastochka, you have no idea what I'm capable of." I tilt her jaw, exposing the long lines of her neck so I can watch her fluttering pulse.

Just a taste, so I know what I'm missing.

My tongue finds the hollow, just above the strand holding her shirt.

I knew she'd be delicious.

Her gasp freezes as my mouth works higher until I pinch the lobe of her ear between my teeth.

"It wouldn't be so bad, wife. You may even enjoy yourself."

When I back away, my dick tents my pants, but I don't make any effort to hide it.

Let her see what she's missing.

"So, dinner?" I slide my thumb under the hem of her alluring shorts. "Or, do I get to have my dessert?"

Her flushed cheeks don't hide the effect I've had. "I'll be down in just a moment."

She darts into her room and slams the door.

I knew she'd see things my way.

8

NADIA

I can't seem to make this chiffon sit right. Cussing at it doesn't seem to help. But, the impending date of my next show means I have to figure this shit out.

Where is my sketchbook? Maybe I had a moment of genius when I was designing.

It isn't where I would expect it to be.

I've taken over one of the extra bedrooms as my new work studio. Trying to get things where I want them is a pain, but it isn't as bad as last week when Roman's goons just dumped everything and I had to spend two days sorting it all out.

I know it's around here somewhere?

Moving piles of fabric, I search on the chair seats I've been using as makeshift racks.

"Dammit." A little flurry of panic begins to percolate through me. That thing is more important than even a journal. It has *everything* in it.

Including personal notes.

But, more importantly for this dress, it has the layout in it.

Argh. This makes me want to pull my hair out. I'm stuck until I find it.

Getting a cup of coffee might help. It will give me a chance to step away and regroup. I need the caffeine. It's going to be a long night until I get everything done for fittings.

Roman is leaning over the counter facing away from me when I come around the corner.

His dark slacks hug the tight curve of his ass and thighs, sending a quiver into my belly as I think about the strength he hides under those snug designer suits.

If I liked him more, I'd be tempted to swat him as I pass and beg for forgiveness.

My stomach drops as I get closer and see what has him so fascinated.

It's my book, full of intimate musings and—

Oh, fuck. Drawings of him.

I think I may puke.

"These are very good." His voice is a growl as he turns the page.

"Um. That's mine." I lunge forward, but grasp empty air as he hoists my hidden secrets above his head and out of my reach.

"Wait, I want to show you my particular favorite." His white button shirt tugs up, exposing his abs and a hint at another tattoo.

I'm torn if I should try and climb the trunk of his body, or stare at the art he's revealed.

Well, the little trail of dark hair that leads below his belt is much more interesting.

He lowers his arm to show me my worst fear.

The picture of him.

"This one. Now I know you've been looking. But, this

part is wrong." He tosses the book onto the counter and begins to unbutton his top.

"What, um. What are you doing?" Snatching my sketches, I hug it to my chest.

Every flavor of embarrassment courses through me as his toned body is slowly revealed.

"Those tattoos, they're all wrong." Peeling the sleeves off, he bares himself. "See? This one." He points at a cluster of skulls beneath a crown. "This one makes grown men piss themselves. You should put it in your drawing."

He moves closer until I'm wedged next to the refrigerator and all I can see is him.

But, I can't resist the beauty in the art.

"It's really well done. What does it mean?" My fingers burn where they trace the ink.

He shrugs. "It means I built my empire on a pile of men. Many have tried to bring down the Petrov family. But, none have succeeded."

His palm covers my wandering hand when I get too close to a smaller mark over his heart.

It's just a date, from almost ten years ago.

"What is that one?" I look up, meeting his dark eyes that are pinched in pain.

"The day our enemies tried to destroy us." He billows his shirt back up over his shoulders and begins to fasten it closed.

He turns away as he opens his belt to stuff the tails inside his waist.

I almost stand on my tiptoes to see what he's hiding.

I've had a hard time sleeping most nights remembering the size of him pressing against my thigh that evening before dinner.

It makes my hands dive beneath my own panties to relieve myself before I can finally drift off.

He glances back and catches me looking.

Heat floods into my cheeks when I turn away.

"Do you want to help me?" He turns with a half smile, the obvious bulge in his open zipper is only covered by the end of the white fabric.

"No. Business, remember?" I let out a long breath. I have to say it to remind myself, even if he's hot as hell and half unclothed.

The grin fades. "Fine. If you don't want to, I'll find someone who will." He buckles his belt and pulls his suit jacket from the back of the chair. "I'm heading to the club. I won't be back for dinner."

"So, what, you move me in, then go out and fuck other women? Nice." I knew he was an asshole from the beginning. I shouldn't be surprised.

But, he's my husband.

Weirdly, even though we aren't like *that*, the thought of him with someone else makes me feel icky.

He pulls his sleeve down and adjusts his cufflinks. One eyebrow raises as he looks at me, his chiseled jaw clenches. "You can come. I have no objections to fucking my wife."

I cling tighter to my book. "Pass," I squeak.

How do I tell him I want him to stay? That I'm just starting to enjoy getting to know him?

But, I'm not ready to be one of his playthings, used and tossed aside.

"As you wish, lastochka." Turning on his Italian shoe heel, he brisks out, leaving nothing but the lingering scent of his cologne.

9

ROMAN

SONG, I'VE BEEN GONE, EX HABIT

https://ffm.to/ivebeengone

Marco and my assistant manager, Violet, rush across the foyer before I can make it to my office.

"Sir, we have an issue." Her bowl-cut mousey brown hair waves with every frantic nod of her head.

"Is this about the renovations on the new club?" The moment Nadia said "I do", I had a crew there getting to work.

I glance at Marco, and he looks just as worried, but shakes his head.

Letting out a big sigh, I push through to my desk. "Alright, let me hear it."

Violet shifts in her loafers. "We've had another, um, 'incident' with Mr. Allen."

"Oh, for fuck's sake. What did he do this time? I swear that man just has a grudge. It isn't our fault his wife came in here and went into a room with four guys." Ever since, he's blamed my club because of his little dick and lack of respect.

"He shut down suite B and C for the weekend. And, we have both of those rooms fully booked." She folds her hands and drops her head.

"How?"

"Well, he, um..." She drifts off and looks up to Marco.

Marco clears his throat before looking at the ceiling before he talks. "He rented them under an alias for an hour session, and then smeared shit everywhere."

I lean back in my chair, letting my palm cover my face. "You have got to be kidding me."

"I wish. The cleaning crew is in B, but they said it's going to take all shift, and they may not finish it." She pushes her glasses up and twists her mouth as she finishes.

"I want posters hung up of that asshole so everyone knows what he looks like." My blood beats in my ears.

Before I left my house I was worked up. Seeing Nadia in that green sundress made it difficult to restrain myself. She has no idea what a thin line she's walking, and how badly I want to make her my wife in every meaning of the word.

The only reason I'm here is to go to one of the free-use rooms and blow off some steam.

This isn't what I wanted to deal with today.

"It sounds like you have everything under control." I'm not in a mindset to think.

That's why I hired them. So I don't have to worry about these things.

Just big ones. Like, how hard my cock is every time I'm in the same room as Nadia.

"I just need your approval for overtime if necessary." Violet slides a form across my desk.

Scribbling my signature across the bottom, I don't

bother to read it. "I'll pay whatever it takes to get those suites up and going. They're cash cows."

Getting the Empire will make dealing with situations like this so much easier. I can shuffle off lower list clients to that location and not have to cancel.

I'm almost there. I've already won half the battle by getting Nadia.

And, her hot body. Full breasts. Begging lower lip...

Fuck.

"If we're done, I have other business to attend to." Standing quickly, I push past Marco through the door, heading for one of the free rooms.

Anyone can go in there and play. Going in means you're open to anything.

I need something to get this raging hard-on to lessen. It's been standing at full attention since my wedding night.

Pushing her against the wall was the worst kind of torture I could have made for myself.

Now I know what she tastes like. How she smells. The way her pulse flutters with my touch.

And how wet my thigh was after it was pressed between her legs.

I pace down the hall like a man possessed.

Because I am, with the thoughts of her.

She's lived in my house for nearly a week. I've never waited this long before.

But, seeing her sketchbook has rekindled a fire I've been trying to keep tamped down.

There's two women and a man in the room when I step in.

They're on their knees between his thighs taking turns using him for a popsicle.

I'm so hard my balls ache. Yet, seeing those two naked

asses sticking up in the air, the seductive smile the one gives me, all I can think is how I would rather it was Nadia.

Maybe if one was wearing a little halter top and shorts?

No. Staring at their writhing bodies makes my dick go soft.

What the hell is wrong with me?

Screw this.

Angrily, I push back to the foyer and into the dark Vegas night.

This club used to be my sanctuary.

All I want now is to be home. Sitting across the table from Nadia, watching her laugh, has suddenly become more satisfying than two bare pussies shoved in the air for me to use at my whim.

I must be broken.

The drive to the house doesn't change my mood.

It's too late for dinner. I'm not hungry for food anyways.

All I can hope for is to stroke off in the shower and hope my cock lets me sleep tonight.

Pausing by her room, I'm tempted to slip inside. I wonder what she'd do if I did?

Would she scream? Or beg me to stay?

My hand rests on the cool metal.

I'm not in the practice of taking what isn't offered. But, she's driving me crazy.

I need a cold fucking shower.

Tugging off my suit jacket, I drape it over my arm as I start to unbutton my shirt.

I'm just about to push in the door to the master suite when I'm stopped by a strange sound.

With one finger, I give it a tap, and it swings open easily.

The sight makes me pause.

Her.

Why is she in my bed?

I don't care. She's naked. And, moaning.

Her bare knees are spread as her hand works between her thighs.

Jesus.

My cock turns to steel in an instant seeing her thrust a purple dildo in and out of herself as she pinches the nipples I *knew* would be perfect.

"It seems my wife has finally decided to join my bed?" I pinch the end of my dick to keep myself from coming in my pants.

I've been thinking of her for days.

Perhaps my patience has paid off.

Her eyes flutter open as her gaze focuses on me. "Oh! I didn't think you'd be home—"

"Don't stop on my account." I toss my blazer on the chair and step close enough to lean against the footboard. "Please. Continue."

She props herself on her elbows with the slick toy in her hand. Her cheeks are cherry red. "I, um. I'm sorry."

"Were you done? Did you come all over my bed?" My words are heavy with restraint. It takes everything in me not to dive my mouth into her sweet cunt and finish her myself.

Her blond hair drapes over her breast as she shakes her head.

"Then do it. I won't touch. I do want to watch, though. So I can dream of you shattering against my pillow." I hold up my palms, not hiding the tent of my pants.

She glances down at my crotch, and it makes my balls throb.

Gritting my teeth, I sit in the chair where my coat rests. "Go on. Rub those rosy nipples for me."

She chews on her lip.

I can see the moment she gives.

Victory almost has me shouting as I see her relax.

"Like this?" One hand trails down her chest and feathers in a small circle around the tight bud.

"Yes. Now, lower." My own nails dig into the soft leather. I've won this round, I don't want to scare her off.

Her knuckle strokes down her smooth belly, making goosebumps pop up in its trail.

What I wouldn't do to lick taste each one before they flatten.

"Good girl." My voice is hoarse with need.

Her tiny gasp is a reward in itself.

"Lower." I can feel the pressure in my own loins building as I watch her.

Tentatively, she pushes two fingers into her wet slit. She spasms as she touches her clit.

"That's it. Flick, baby."

Every movement of her hand feels like it's threaded into my cock, which twitches in time with her.

I can hear her panting. With every breath, it grows louder until I almost feel the heat running over me.

Her heels dig into the mattress as she grinds against her palm.

"Put that rubber dick in, lastochka. Ride it like it's me fucking you."

Her chin turns so she can see me.

Those chocolate eyes latch onto mine as she slowly penetrates herself in a long push. "Like that?"

This woman. I can't decide if this is heaven or hell.

"Yes, wife. Almost out, then fast and deep." Tightening in my gut tells me I'm close.

Her mouth forms an 'o' as she obeys.

"Faster." Squeezing my fists makes them ache, but I need the distraction.

She's just so damned beautiful.

Driving that toy in and out of her pussy, she raises her ass to meet each thrust.

I can see her stomach clenching.

"Twirl that hard clit one more time for me." My balls seize as she screams.

Her toes push out until her body is a rainbow over my blanket, locked into a climax that has tears squeezing from her.

My own pelvis gives in, shuddering me into a full release in my boxers.

I didn't even have to touch myself.

She drops, spent, onto the comforter, one arm propped over her face. "My, god," she moans.

I'm afraid to move. I know I made a mess, but I don't want to ruin this gift she has given me.

When I feel dripping down my thigh, I give in and stand.

"Did you enjoy that? You have no idea how much more I could show you if you'd let me." I don't give her a chance to answer, but go into the bathroom to clean myself up.

I'm finished when I hear my phone ring from the pocket of my jacket, still draped across the best seat in the house.

10

NADIA

I can't believe I did that.

But, maybe I'm glad I did.

What a way to tell him I'm interested then having him catch me naked in his bed?

I've never come that hard before in my life. Why was it so hot with him sitting there telling me what to do?

I think he enjoyed the show. His fists were squeezed so tightly, I thought he was going to break them.

And when he instructed me, my mind was free.

But, now the embarrassment of what I did is catching up.

While he's in the bathroom, I throw on my robe and am just about out of his room when his phone rings.

Does he always get calls this late?

"Hello, Violet." His voice is husky as he answers.

Who is Violet?

His dark eyes burn into me as he listens to whatever it is she's saying.

"Of course, I'll be there right away. Don't do anything until I get there." He clicks his cell off.

I feel all kinds of awkward. Should I leave? What just happened?

"Do you have to go?" I whisper. My hand tugs the robe tighter around me.

He saunters over and leans against the wall, crowding me with his body. "That depends? Do you want me to stay?"

I don't get it. Is this a choice? If I say no, he runs off to another woman?

If I say yes, am I crossing a line that I may regret?

I chew on my lip in indecision and watch his dark eyes narrow before he pulls away.

"You're right, Nadia. This is just a business deal." He gathers his suit coat from the chair and slides it over his broad shoulders.

My stomach drops. He might as well have dumped a bucket of cold water over me.

"Yes. Business," I echo. I feel sick.

"Remember that." He winks and disappears.

I'm frozen as I hear his footsteps fade down the hall.

It's only when the main door shuts that it snaps me out.

The nerve on that guy!

He watched me! He talked me through the most intimate thing I think I've *ever* done.

And then, just leaves?

The shock morphs into anger.

I can't believe him. Running away to someone else?

He's my husband!

Who owns a sex club.

I hate how turned on I was by him watching me.

And how used I feel now.

Well. Screw him. I can find someone who won't leave

me begging. There has to be some guy at that club who will want to get me off.

I can't believe I'm even considering this, but being around him has woken up a spark in me I wasn't even aware I was missing.

A fully functioning sex drive.

I thought it was me. Turns out, I just didn't want to fuck my ex.

11

ROMAN

SONG, KOOL-AID, BRING ME THE HORIZON.

Dragging myself away from Nadia is one of the hardest things I've had to do.

I know she wants more from me, I just know she would be the perfect fit for me.

A woman who has control of her life but wants it taken away in the bedroom. To me, she could be the missing piece of the puzzle.

It feels right and I want more, yet something is stopping me. My own ego perhaps.

Kicking open the door to my office, I find a flustered Violet tapping away on the computer.

"Have they gone?"

She pulls up the security feeds and chews on her long purple nail.

"Rico is dealing with them now."

I roll up my sleeves and sit on the couch, letting out an exasperated sigh as I tip my head back against the wall.

I didn't need to be here, I could have fucked Nadia seven ways to Sunday. Fuck, right this second my dick could have been deep inside her.

"Did you want a room, Sir?" Violet's soft voice shakes me out of my dirty thoughts of my wife.

I shake my head, looking down at my Rolex.

Nadia will probably still be awake, maybe there is a chance to show her still tonight.

"No. I have plans with my wife."

Luckily I have a whole room of equipment to use on her at home. I can see how far she can be pushed.

Maybe I'll start her off on the bench. Or the cross.

No, I can't wait to have her strapped to my bed, her ass in the air and at my mercy. I'll spank it until it's red, then rub her down until she screams, begging to come.

"I think she might have other plans, Roman."

I pull my head back, confusion taking over, until my eyes lock on the monitor.

I can't help the grin that spreads on my lips.

She has balls.

"Tell Nic to let her in. Everyone knows the rules here."

It's simple, you don't touch the boss' wife. You do, you die.

Resting my hand on the back of her chair, I lean over and don't take my eyes off Nadia. A short little black dress that hugs her toned frame beautifully. Paired with gold heels and a matching bag.

No wonder every guy's head has turned the moment she makes it through the double doors.

I can almost taste her on my tongue. By far, the most stunning woman to walk into this building, and my life.

She slowly approaches the bar, looking far more relaxed than I have ever seen her. Which worries me.

She's mine.

I'll do whatever I have to to remind her of that fact.

My ring, my wife, only ever mine to please.

"Are you in deep with her?" Violet asks, not looking at me.

I swallow the lump in my throat.

"It appears that way,"

A fire spreads through my chest, an unfamiliar feeling, as Vlad pulls up alongside her. He's close, far too close to her for my liking.

Clenching my fists, I study her reaction to him.

He whispers something in her ear and my frustration grows.

And then she smiles at him and nods and I nearly explode with rage as he laces his fingers through hers and guides her into the gold room.

"Mother fucker," I grit out under my breath, my hand going for my gun.

"Want me to fix this?" Violet says I almost can't hear her under the blood pounding in my ears.

The door closes behind them.

I have two choices, I let her explore without me and I lose her.

Or, I show them both who is in charge.

I'll play her game.

There will only be one of us coming out of that room victorious though.

And I certainly won't lose my wife to a sub I trained. He knows the rules, and now I shall remind everyone of what happens when you cross a Petrov.

"No. I will sort this out myself. Turn the security footage off outside the room." I demand, heading for the door.

"Do you need—"

I hold up my finger to cut her off with a simple answer.

"Yes. One hour."

12

NADIA

SONG, I KNOW (FADED), EX HABIT

https://ffm.to/iknowfaded

I let out a gasp as my new friend Vlad pushes me face first against the wall. His hot breath beats against my shoulder as his fingers find the zipper on the side of my dress.

"We are going to get in so much trouble for this."

My blood runs cold as he presses his mouth on my skin. I wish this was Roman holding me in place, his lips on my body. I half expect him to barge in and whisk me away.

But, that won't happen. We aren't really married. His words echo through my mind. Business deal. I thought that was what I wanted.

Vlad spins me around to meet his green eyes and unbuttons his shirt to reveal his six pack. Roman's is better and covered in tattoos. Vlad discards his shirt on the floor, his erection tenting his slacks as he closes the distance.

His palm brushes against my cheek, I close my eyes as he leans in. I picture Roman in my mind as I return his kiss.

He jerks back as the door crashes open and my eyes go

wide. My heart nearly pounds out of my chest as my husband strides through the entrance as if he owns it.

His gaze locks with mine and I hold my breath, Vlad stays silent, bowing his head to look at the ground. Roman doesn't look at me as he reaches Vlad, tips his chin up and their noses almost touch. I have to clench my thighs together, damn, the two of them that close are hot.

Almost like the scene I read the other day. I wonder if...

"One rule, Vlad. You broke it and you know the consequences."

Vlad nods, his Adam's apple bobbing as he swallows.

Slowly, Roman turns to face me, I expect fury in his eyes, but it isn't there. What is there could be worse for me... pure, raw, hunger.

With his hand on Vlad's shoulder, he pushes him to his knees and Vlad keeps his eyes to the ground. I watch in fascination.

"Did you really think I'd let another man fuck my wife and not join in?"

A blush creeps up my neck, setting me on fire.

My mouth falls open as Roman slides off his belt and wraps it around his fist.

"I think it's time I taught you both a valuable lesson. In here, you're mine to fuck as I please."

Both of us?

A smirk creeps up on his lips as he pulls Vlad's head up by his blond hair.

My heart is racing and my pussy is throbbing.

Roman unzips himself, freeing his massive cock, leaving it in front of Vlad's mouth. Roman keeps his eyes on me as he pushes Vlad's face closer to his dick.

"Be a good girl and spread your legs, then play with

yourself. You'll want to get yourself ready to take both of us."

My breath catches in my throat and Roman's eyes burn into mine.

"Don't make me ask again," he hisses.

I let out a gasp as Vlad wraps his lips around Roman's huge cock.

How the hell is this so damn hot? Watching two guys?

I can't tear my eyes from them as I dip my hand under my dress and run it along my soaking slit. I don't think I have ever been this wet in my life.

"I can hear how ready you're getting watching another man suck off your husband."

I nod, sliding two fingers in. As my eyes flutter closed I can feel Roman's stare on me.

"Eyes open, baby. You watch this. It will only ever happen tonight."

I do as he says. Romans jaw is tight as he fucks Vlad's mouth violently.

In one swift motion, he tears Vlad off and stalks towards me.

He grabs me by the throat, almost lifting me off my feet.

"Is this what you really want? Both of us?"

I hesitate, looking between him and Vlad. My teeth sink into my lower lip as Roman's crash over mine. I moan into his mouth. I want him.

But, I want him to show me everything. Seeing him with Vlad turned me on so hard I can't miss this opportunity.

"You are going to be the perfect little slut for me, Nadia," he whispers.

His fingers tighten around my throat making my head fuzzy.

"She's fucking beautiful, Rom. I can't wait to taste her."

A darkness flashes across Roman's eyes. Was that jealousy?

"We do this once, and once only. I'll give you what you want and then you're mine. Understand?"

He pins my hands above my head with one hand and pushes back open my thighs.

"Do you understand?" he grunts out.

"Yes, fuck yes, Roman."

"Good girl."

His hand slides under my panties and he thrusts his fingers deep inside.

"So fucking wet for me."

Just as a moan escapes me, he pulls them out and steps back, looking over at Vlad still on his knees.

"You will both submit to me. Neither of you so much as moves without my say so. Is that clear?"

"Yes, sir," Vlad quickly replies.

I raise an eyebrow at Roman. Has he been with guys before?

Roman chuckles, walking over to Vlad.

"Stand and take your clothes off," he commands.

"And you," he says, locking eyes with me before turning his attention to Vlad, who immediately does as he says.

I let out a gasp as Roman grabs him by the back of his head, wraps his hand around Vlad's cock and presses his lips over his as he starts to pump him.

Holy fuck. It's so hot.

The entire roam is scorching, listening to them moan into each other's mouths.

Jesus.

He whispers something into Vlad's ear and he groans in

response. They both turn to look at me making a blush run up my neck.

"Tell me, lastochka. This is your fantasy. What do you want?"

My eyes zone in on Roman stroking Vlad's cock, swiping the pre-cum from the tip. I want to feel them both, but I want Roman to consume me. He's the one I want more than anything right now.

But, I also want to watch him in control of Vlad. I want to see him come apart. I want it all. If it's for one night only.

"I want you both to fuck me, at the same time." I pause, taking a breath, remembering how turned on that book had me.

"And I want you to fuck him."

Romans lips twist up into a grin.

"My wife gets whatever she wants." He shrugs, and tears off his white shirt.

My body ignites as Roman walks over to me and lifts me into his arms, crashing his lips over mine, sinking his fingers in so I'm completely full and stretched around him.

"Tell me to stop and I will, if it is too much, it ends. You are in control too, okay?"

"Yes," I whisper.

"Yes, what?" His face is stern.

"Yes, sir."

He kisses me again. "See? My perfect girl."

He unclasps my bra, letting it fall to the floor before he leans down and sucks my nipple. Dropping me down on the center of the plush bed, he pushes my legs apart and settles between them.

Holding up a finger, he motions for Vlad to join.

He does, licking his lips as he approaches us.

"Where do you want me, sir?"

My legs tighten around Roman's waist. Nerves suddenly take over. Can I really handle both of them? Will this ruin whatever the hell it was with Roman?

"It's okay, baby. I've got you, you're mine," he whispers.

"Lay next to Nadia. She wants to suck your cock, don't you, gorgeous?"

He brushes my hair away from my face.

I glance over at Vlad spread on the bed and nod.

"I do."

"On all fours. You might have his cock in your mouth, but I am going to fuck you so hard while you suck him that you'll have no choice but to remember you belong to me, wife."

Roman positions himself behind me as I get on my knees between Vlad's legs. Grabbing hold of me by the hair, he guides my mouth over Vlad's cock and I take him in my mouth. I moan around his girth as Roman sinks inside of me, slapping my ass as he ups the pace.

"Look at you two, fucking perfect," he growls behind me.

I take Vlad as deep as I can go.

"Fuck, your mouth is sinful," Vlad groans.

I hear Roman grunt behind me. He presses down on my back, spreading my ass apart. I feel his warm spit run between my cheeks. I almost scream when his finger slides in slowly.

"You like it full?"

"Y-yes." My words are muffled by Vlad's cock.

"Good. Wait till you've got two of us fucking you."

Blood thumps in my ears at the thought. I look up through my lashes at Vlad, he's grinning at me.

Roman stiffens behind me, shouting out my name as he

spills inside. As he pulls out, I feel his cum dripping down my legs. I squeal as he picks me up and tosses me down on my back on the bed, pushing open my knees, a fire in his eyes as he looks between my legs.

"Fuck, your pussy is overflowing. All swollen and pink." He runs a hand over his jaw and looks to Vlad.

"Clean up my wife. Lick up every drop of me."

Vlad scrambles onto his knees and positions himself between my thighs. I grab onto his hair as he feasts, but I don't stop looking at Roman, who winks at me, stepping behind Vlad's ass.

"Look at you both, being so fucking good for me." He slaps Vlad's hip and I feel him moan against my sensitive pussy. He licks circles around my clit, before moving down and licking along my thighs.

"You taste so good," Vlad says, looking up at me before twisting his head to Roman.

"Both of you do." He continues and I tip my head back in pure bliss as he sucks on me.

Roman leans over him and pushes the back of Vlad's head so he dives deeper into my pussy and I yell out as he sucks my clit.

"If you're going to eat out my wife, do it properly. Make her scream."

In the back of my head I'm imagining Roman's mouth on me.

Roman steps around to the edge of the bed and sits up on his knees, his huge dick in my face.

"Suck me clean."

Without hesitating, I give him the best blow job of my life. His hands circle around my throat and he squeezes.

"You're so close aren't you?"

I know he is, too. I can feel his thighs tensing. My legs start to shake next to Vlad's head.

Without warning, Roman positions himself over my face, I tip my head back so his cock is back in my mouth. Holding up his weight with his arm, he starts to lick my clit as Vlad's strong hands lifts my hips slightly and starts to fuck me with his tongue.

Holy fucking shit.

Both of them eat me like they're starved, and Roman's cock hits the back of my throat. My head starts to spin and my body erupts, I see stars as a violent climax tears through me.

I dig my nails into Roman's ass and my hips buck on their own accord.

Before I can even catch my breath, Roman rolls off me and Vlad sits up on his knees. In my post-orgasm haze, I watch as Roman leans over and strokes Vlad's cock. Positioning himself next to him, with his other hand he grabs his jaw and slams his lips over his.

"Fuck, my wife tastes so good on your tongue."

I sit up on my knees, and join them, waiting for Roman's command. I might not know much about this lifestyle, but I am picking up on the fact I only do as he says. It is so freeing, not having to think, just feel.

Roman threads his fingers through my hair and drags me to join their kiss. All three of our tongues mesh together, a mixture of mine and Roman's taste, and our moans fill the room. I'm in the middle of two, huge, powerful men.

"Feel both of us, baby," Roman mutters against my cheek.

I grab each of their cocks in either hand and begin to slowly stroke them at the exact same pace. Inching open my legs so they both can start playing. I can't tell whose fingers are where. But fuck, it feels so good.

Vlad moves himself forward, both of them groaning into my mouth as I work them.

"I want you both in me," I whisper in Romans' mouth.

13

ROMAN

SONG, LIKE U, ROSENFELD

"You'll have to beg for that, baby."

Her hips rock against my fingers as I plunge them inside.

"Beg. Me. For. It."

Her head tips back. I can't resist leaning in and sucking on her throat. She pumps my cock harder and Vlad's hand covers hers.

I let out a throaty groan. That jealousy is still burning in the background. I'm holding it back, for her.

And quite honestly, it is fucking hot.

"Please, Roman."

Her little breathy cry has me almost panting.

"Try again, lastochka," I growl against her lips.

Vlad runs his tongue along her throat.

I yank back his head and cover my lips over his. Tasting myself and Nadia all over his mouth.

"Please, sir? I need this. I need your cocks filling me. I want this so much. Please?"

I grin against Vlad's lips.

He's a good sub. It's a shame he had to touch what's mine.

But after this, I'm hers. There will be no one else for me.

"I thought you wanted to watch me fuck him?" I ask her, raising an eyebrow.

She bites down on her plump bottom lip. "Oh, I do."

My hand shoots out and grabs her by the throat, pulling her up.

Her eyes go wide as I squeeze. I'm on the cusp of losing control.

"Come on, sir. Let me feel her."

I clench my fist as his hands wrap around my cock.

"You get her ass prepped." I turn to a red faced Nadia. "You, on your back, knees up to your chest." I point at the bed.

Without hesitating, she does as I say. Her glistening cunt is ready for me.

I let Vlad position himself between her legs, stroking my cock as I watch him feast, fingering her at the same time.

I could do it better.

I lock my eyes to Nadia's, watching her reaction. She holds her breath as he sinks one finger in her tight hole.

"Breathe for me, baby," I say softly.

"Keep a finger in her pussy and suck on her clit," I command him.

"That's it, good girl." I bend down, so my lips brush her cheek and I kiss her with everything I have.

Proving to her who she really belongs to. She might have another guy tongue fucking and pumping her ass.

But, she's mine. I allowed this.

"What do you say? You ready?" I whisper against her lips.

She nervously nods her head as I cup her cheeks.

"I'll do it first, baby. I've got you. You'll always be safe with me."

And I mean every word.

Vlad moves to the side so I can position myself between her legs. I roll a condom onto my cock, then squirt some lube on it and let Vlad rub it along my shaft.

I lift her hips and run the head down, before rimming the hole with the tip.

"Relax, baby."

She hisses as I slowly sink inside. I rub small circles on her clit to distract her as her tight ass takes my cock.

"Eyes on me."

They snap to mine and my heart races. I up the pace and sink a finger into her pussy.

Vlad bends over and looks up at me as he licks her pussy. Nadia's dainty hand pumps his dick.

"She's delicious, sir. You're lucky."

I close my eyes as her tight ass strangles my cock so tight.

Every moan she lets out is my name. Fuck, it's hot.

Vlad works his tongue back, catching my shaft as I push in her ass and out.

"This is so hot, Rom," she says breathlessly.

As I look up, she's smiling at me, blowing her hair out of her face in pure bliss.

That's all I care about.

"Damn right, baby. You're doing so well."

She wants us both. She can have us.

Reluctantly I pull out and rip the used cover off of me. I'm almost breathless. I lay down next to her and lift her to straddle me.

I pull her down by the throat, offering her ass to Vlad as I thrust inside her tight cunt.

Her lips find mine and my fingers tighten around her throat. She screams into my mouth as he grabs her ass and pushes himself in.

"How does it feel?" I rasp against her lips.

"So fucking good, Rom. Thank you," she moans.

I can hear Vlad telling me how good her ass feels.

I know.

And it's *mine.*

His balls slap against me with each thrust, I keep her held in place as we continue to fuck her within an inch of her life.

"You're perfect, lastochka. Taking us both like the good little slut I knew you could be."

I feel Vlad pull away and his warm cum spills over us as he pumps himself. I keep fucking her, my fingers replacing his cock in her ass. Matching the rhythm of my thrusts.

I feel her start to tremble against me.

"Come for me, only for me, baby."

She cries out, her pussy tightening around me and I follow her over the edge, her name on my lips as I fill her up.

My breathing is heavy as she sits up. Vlad is next to us and she turns to look at him, my dick twitches inside her as he grabs her face. I give him a nod and he kisses her, she rolls her hips on me.

Shit. I'm already hard again.

I slide my fingers up his thigh and stroke his cock.

"Your turn. My wife wants to watch me fuck you."

She climbs off me. I swipe the cum from between her legs and shove my fingers in her mouth.

Turning my attention to Vlad, his eyes light up as I approach him.

Rubbing my hands over Nadia's soaked cunt, mixed with mine and her, I push him forwards so his head is buried in the mattress and smother his asshole in our cum, stroking him as I do.

I keep my eyes locked on Nadia's. Trying to gauge what she's thinking as I lean over to the bedside drawer, pull out a condom and roll it over my shaft.

I'm not sure how many women want to watch their husbands fuck another man.

To me, it's another tight fucking hole. I don't care. I break in a lot of subs here.

I point to Nadia and motion to her to spread her legs. Like a good girl she does nice and wide with a wicked grin.

I need to see that sweet pussy when I sink into his ass.

Positioning myself behind him, I drizzle myself with lube, I spread his ass apart and thrust inside him.

Jesus.

It does feel good.

He cries out into the covers and I fuck him like an animal. So hard it would hurt.

And he loves it.

He tugs on his own dick at the same time. Nadia has her mouth open, watching me with pure desire in her chocolate eyes.

I blow her a kiss before plowing back into him. My hands grip on his cheeks, I let out a grunt.

"More, sir," he whines into the pillow.

I hiss, that word spurring me on further.

I push down on the top of his back, kicking his legs out further so I can sink in as deep as I can go.

"Nadia, here," I grit.

I want her.

"On your front, lay on his back and butt in the air."

She does exactly as I say, I grab her perfect ass, lifting it up enough I can lean forward and smother my face in her sweet pussy.

The taste of her on my tongue brings me closer to climax. Hearing her moans, feeling her quiver on my tongue. Damn, she is perfect.

But I want her to get me off.

I pull out of Vlad, catching my breath.

"Both of you, on your knees, center of the bed."

A smile is on my lips as they scramble into position, Vlad looks like he's about to explode and Nadia is dripping down her thighs.

I position myself in front of Vlad, our throbbing cocks next to each other.

"You finish us off, baby. At the same time."

Rolling off my condom, I toss it onto the floor and let out a groan as I feel her fingers wrap around us both.

I place my hand over hers and guide her, so she strokes us together.

When I glance over to Vlad with a grin, he's looking like he's trying his hardest not to come until I grant him permission.

"Make us come so I can have you to myself again," I mutter against her lips.

She nods and works faster. A low groan escapes me and my body tenses up, I can't take more. Grabbing her thigh, I work my palm up and cup her pussy, sinking two digits inside her. She moans into my mouth and that is enough.

"Now." I force out the word as I cum all over her wrist and his dick, kissing her until I almost can't breathe. I hear Vlad panting and cursing under his breath until his warm seed spills out over my dick.

I keep kissing her and fucking her with my fingers until

she tips over the edge, shuddering against me and eventually falling into my arms.

I sit back on my heels and pull her against my chest, closing my eyes and nuzzling into her neck.

"You are perfect, Nadia," I whisper just for her.

Holding her tightly, I look up to Vlad.

"You're done now," I say to him.

He knew how this would end.

Every man in here knew the rules.

You touch my wife, you die.

He's lucky he got to taste her before he goes to hell.

Leaning over, I grab my silenced Sig Sauer from my jacket pocket laying over the chair, and nod to him to get off the bed.

He backs away, his arms raising. "No! I didn't know—"

I pull the trigger. The bullet hits between the eyes and he thumps to the floor. Nadia jumps, but I hold her tighter. Even as she tries to get out of my arms, I don't let up.

And, right on time, the door opens and an unamused Rico strolls in. I grab the comforter and pull it over Nadia as he looks between me and the dead body. I shrug at him with a grin.

Turning us away, I release her and quickly grab her by both cheeks to stop her from looking behind. Fear dances in her eyes and it makes my cock twitch.

"What did I tell you, lastochka?"

She goes to speak, her bottom lip quivering.

I grab her chin between my fingers, forcing her to look at me. Maybe she does need to see the real monster I am. It makes no difference, she is never leaving me.

I let go and she turns her head and gasps. She tries to scramble off the bed in a panic, I hook my arms around her waist dragging her back to me. I glance over as my men are moving Vlad's body out of the door. It slams shut behind them.

"He knew the rules, and he still wanted a taste. This is who I am and you are fucking mine."

I lift her into my arms and take us into the shower, closing the door behind me.

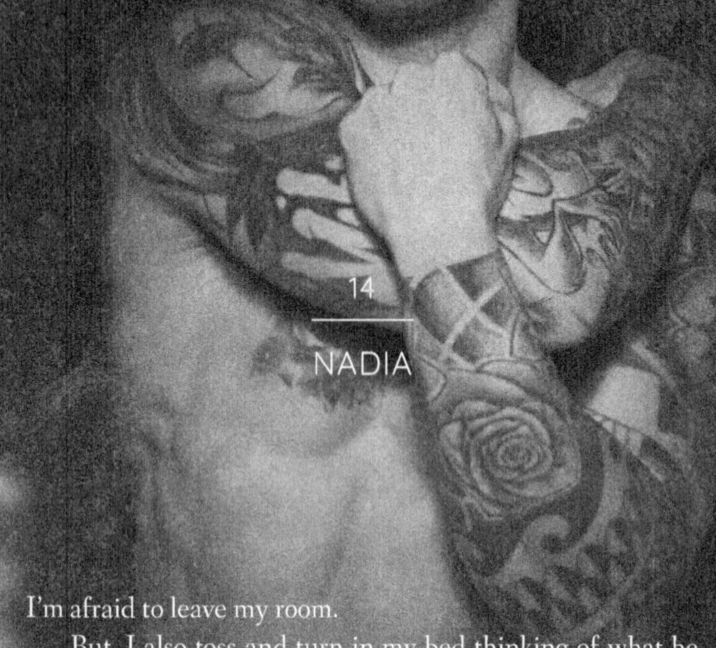

14

NADIA

I'm afraid to leave my room.

But, I also toss and turn in my bed thinking of what he felt like.

This battle within me is all losers and no winners.

My husband is a really bad man. He killed someone because of *me*. While I was in the room.

It makes me feel weird. Appalled, and turned on.

And, also intimidated. Would he hurt me? He hasn't shown any signs, in fact, the complete opposite.

He *murdered* someone.

Yet, I can't stop thinking about him. I want him more than ever. I need him to show me what he can do to me. He's right. I had a taste of it and I am craving more.

My books don't have the same appeal, not after I've experienced the real thing.

Reality is so much better than fiction. But, these stories keep the memories so vivid, I can't stop reading them.

Why does this have to be this complicated? Is this really the life I want? A man who takes care of me, fucks me any way I beg, and kills for me?

God, when I frame it like that, he sounds perfect.

I just need some time to think. I have a big show coming up, and that's where I should be focusing my efforts.

Not on how big his cock is.

Or, how good he felt when he fucked my ass. How many times did I get off? Three? Four?

A wave of heat smothers my cheeks. Did I really do that? I've always scoffed at it in the romance books. Never thought it could be real.

It should feel wrong, but there's a part of me that craves more.

"So? You've been M.I.A. for days. What's going on? Are you going to be ready for the show?" Rochelle's raspy voice is a welcome distraction.

"Things are just, well, complicated." How do I tell her what happened?

I don't.

Is this a test? Is he somehow making me choose him or the right thing?

"I know that sound. That's the sigh of the freshly fucked." Her laughter tinges on a cough. "I thought you weren't marrying him for *that?*"

"I didn't. It just kind of...happened." I can't hide it from her forever.

Her cackle makes me smile. "Like, an accident? Driving along and bumped uglies on the freeway?"

"Um. More like I ran into him and got rear-ended." I can feel the fire over my face enflame.

She sounds like she's choking. "Jesus, girl! You can't just drop that kind of juice on me! I'm gonna die of diabetes from all that sugar!"

I'm laughing so hard I snort. "It was a pretty wild time," I admit.

"Wild? My idea of that is when my cat gets the zoomies. You went full on safari level." A fanning noise waves through the speaker.

I can just imagine her sitting there with a piece of paper fluttering it in front of her face.

A loud knock startles me.

It's him.

"He's here. I'll call you back later." My heart beats faster knowing he's so close.

"Girl, go. Fill me in when I see you. I want *all* the details!" she shrieks before I hang up.

What am I going to do?

15

ROMAN

I know I scared her, but this is getting ridiculous.

She's been locked up in her room, or off at work, every moment.

Dinner has only been in passing.

And, I can't stop thinking about how tight her pussy is and how good it felt squeezing my cock.

I want to do it again.

Until we're both too exhausted to move.

But, I don't know how long I can drag this out.

I always go after what I want, and I want my wife... for keeps, not a business deal.

I am impressed she hasn't called the cops. Maybe she knows that it's futile. Or, perhaps deep down, she doesn't want me to go to jail.

That's a tiny bubble of hope.

Before I give in and finish our contract, I want a chance to rectify the situation.

After making a few phone calls, I find myself outside of her room.

"Go away, Roman." Her voice calls through the thick wood of the door.

"I have a request of my wife. Come out to dinner with me tonight? Wear your favorite outfit that you designed, please." I can't hear anything.

"Why should I?" She has a petulant sound to her question.

Enough I have the urge to spank it out of her.

"I want to show the world my beautiful bride at least during our marriage. Then, I promise we will get the papers signed." It's the last thing I want to do, now that I've had a taste of her.

She's been asking ever since the night I made her mine in the club.

The last thing I want is to let her go. But, strangely, I have this drive within me to do anything to make her happy, even if it's letting her leave.

I don't know what she's done to me. It isn't like me to put anyone else's desires over my own.

This must have been the wrong idea.

She hasn't answered. I guess she's already signed me off.

It's crazy, but the other night, I really felt like there was something between us.

Should I have killed that guy? Yep. He touched what's mine.

In hindsight, I shouldn't have let her see.

But, proving the point was half the reason I did.

I'm nearly out of the hall when I hear her door open.

"Okay, what time?" Her blond hair is in a messy bun on the top of her head with tendrils fanning around her face.

My fingers tingle with the urge to tangle them in her locks and pull her to me.

"Seven tonight." A knot forms in my belly as a giddy feeling spreads through my limbs.

One more chance.

SPECTER IS an elite VIP club at the pinnacle of Vegas. The ride up in the external glass elevators gives a breathtaking view of the lights of the city.

But, I only have eyes for Nadia. Her stunning beauty is showcased in a soft lavender dress that shimmers in opalescence every time she moves.

The low cut in the front is both revealing and discreet. It makes me want to throw my jacket around her, but proudly strut with her on my arm. It's hard to concentrate with her so close. Her heat radiates through my clothes and burns into my sides as she hugs herself tightly to me when the maitre d approaches.

"Right this way, Mr. Petrov." He bows slightly, extending his arm in a broad gesture to the thinly spaced tables.

Powerful people dine here, and pay handsomely for the luxury of privacy. And, I bought the best seat in the house tonight.

"Is that... Is that Elizabeth Devonson?" Nadia whispers as her hand wraps within my elbow.

"Who?" Leaning closer, I silently beg her lips to draw nearer to my ear.

Her warm breath tickles over my skin as she repeats herself.

"Why is she important?" I know exactly who she is.

She cost me a small fortune to make an appearance tonight.

"She's, well, um." Nadia's cheeks flood with pink when her eyes land on Elizabeth chatting quietly with a friend. "She's the most famous designer in Paris right now. Her style with silk and chiffon has set the world on *fire!*" Nadia turns, her eyes wide with excitement clinging to me.

"Has it?" I pull her closer, letting my palm hug her hip as we walk. "Would you like to meet her?"

Her fingers dig into me. "No! I'd be too embarrassed!" Crimson covers her throat, tempting me to chase it with my tongue.

"Don't be silly. She would be the lucky one for meeting you, lastochka." Tugging her with me, we find our spot on an elevated platform in the back of the restaurant.

Everyone can see us silhouetted against the Vegas skyline.

But, they seem dim and dull in comparison to my beautiful wife. She's becoming the shining light to me, the beacon drawing me through each day with the hopes of catching a glimpse of her through the darkness.

She bites her lip and gives me a small smile before I pull her chair and beckon her to sit.

"Thank you, Roman." Her dark eyes watch me take the seat before her, and don't leave mine as I lean across the narrow table.

"I'm the one who should be thanking you for offering me another chance to spend some time with you." I don't want to add the words 'before we part' because they seem so final.

Looking down, she fusses with her napkin until the waiter approaches to take our order.

When she does glance at me again, her brows are furrowed and the corner of her mouth drops into a small frown. "Did you bring the papers?"

I can't tell if that's hope or resignation in her sigh when I nod.

"Excuse me?" A high voice approaches us.

Just in time.

"Are you Nadia Sanders?" Elizabeth Devonson steps closer, her smile is broad and genuine appearing.

She must be quite happy with the funds I offered.

Nadia's cheeks flush with bright red. "I-I am."

Elizabeth brushes her bushy green hair back with an embellished wave. "I was just telling my friend, I couldn't believe it was you! I saw your show in L.A. this past fall and have been absolutely dying to meet you!" Bracelets jangle on her wrists as she clasps Nadia's hand enthusiastically.

"You were there?" Nadia stares up with wide eyes as she chews on her bottom lip.

"I would never forget the sequins on that wrap!" she squeals and claps her palms. "When I saw Roman walk in, I was wondering who would be lucky enough to be on his arm. Imagine my wondrous surprise when I saw who it was! I swear you're the only one in the world talented enough to be with him."

Elizabeth steps back and tugs a quiet dark haired man closer. "This is my husband, Reggie. We should all get together for dinner one of these days!"

A frown furrows her sleek brows. "Wait, are you two a thing?" She flicks her long painted nail between us.

This is my chance.

I lean forward and take Nadia's hand in mine. "She's my wife."

Watching Nadia, I catch the glimmer of a shy smile as the blush works her way up her neck.

"Marvelous! Cause for celebration! Roman, you never

put out an announcement? Did I miss the party?" She playfully smacks my shoulder.

"We eloped," Nadia says quietly before biting her lip.

"Oh, that's so romantic!" Elizabeth clasps her fingers to her chest, her bracelets slide down nearly to her elbows. "Roman lent me some of his models last year for a show. We absolutely have to collab, girl. Call me, and we can set up a show the likes of which Vegas can only dream of!" Her puffy dress swirls around her before she pulls her silent husband with her down the steps of the dias.

Well, that went better than expected.

Nadia watches her leave, her large eyes practically unblinking until Elizabeth disappears.

"I can't believe you know her. She's so, so amazing." Her sigh slumps her onto her chair.

She looks happy for the first time in a week.

"You know, I'm not a bad man. I just don't want anyone touching what's mine." I stab my fork into my carbonara and then hold the morsel up to emphasize myself. "And, you are. As long as you wear that ring." I gesture to her left hand wrapped around her wine flute.

She lifts her arm, twirling the diamond around her dainty digit. "I get that, now."

I half expect her to pull it off, but she twists it back to show off its full glory.

That may be a good sign.

It's a whole different kind of high being able to tell everyone she belongs to me. The shiny stone is just a tiny representation of how much she's grown to mean to me.

I never expected to want her as badly as I do.

As the dessert dishes are cleared, I pull out the papers she wants so badly to sign.

The ones adding me to the deed.

Just a single step after this clears.

Divorce.

My stomach rolls at the thought of her leaving. But, I can't force her to stay. I'm not like the Kosovich family that tried so hard to ruin us.

Marriage by force doesn't exist under my father's laws.

Nor mine.

Her face pales as she picks up her pen. "How long until this is finalized?" she whispers.

The tip hovers over the surface shakily.

Is she reluctant to sign?

"Just a few more weeks." I wish it was forever.

She swallows hard before scratching her name on the line.

I don't know why, but it feels like the air got thicker and heavy on my shoulders.

The countdown is on.

"Can we please go?" She looks up, and I swear I see the sheen of tears in her eyes.

"Of course." Giving her my hand, I help her rise from her chair and tug her close.

I want to feel her against me as long as she lets me.

16

NADIA

SONG, ON YOUR KNEES, EX HABIT

https://ffm.to/onknees

I've locked myself away from him for the night. Dinner was too much, it all felt... too real. Every time I look into his deep brown eyes, I get lost, yet find myself at the same time.

The idea of our future together, the fear of letting him have my heart only for him to crush it.

But, he's the first man to really tap into the true me.

He's opened up a part of me I've buried deep for so long, the part of me that felt ashamed.

Rolling over to my side, I pick up my kindle from the night stand.

I'm no further than I was the day Roman knocked and came to my house. I have no desire to finish this. Not when I know I have my own book boyfriend, or fake husband rather, on the other side of this door.

A man who would kill for me.

A man who can unlock every desire I never thought possible.

But can this man love me as fiercely?

My eyes roam over the page. Ah, yes, the MMF. My body starts to burn up as I take in the words, not from them though, from my own experience flashing back in my mind.

Remember how it felt to be under Roman's full control.

I'm so wrapped up in my thoughts of him, I've skipped two pages and have to go back.

"What is wrong with me," I groan, throwing my arm over my face.

I'm turned on, mildly terrified of my fake husband, but also am desperate for him to storm through that door, lift me into his arms and rail me so hard I can't walk.

More than that, I want to know everything about this man. I want his heart as much as I want his massive cock.

I manage to get myself through two more chapters, they don't have their usual effect on me. Just as I'm about to give up and call it a night there is a heavy knock on the door before it crashes open.

I sit up, pulling the blanket up to my neck and bite down on my lip as Roman strides through in his gray sweatpants and black tee.

"This is driving me crazy, lastochka." There is almost disbelief in his words.

I raise an eyebrow at him.

"What is Roman?" I whisper, not trusting my own voice.

He steps to the side of the bed, towering over me. His eyes flick to the kindle.

"Knowing my wife is in here, on her own, when she should be being looked after in her husband's bed."

"That wasn't part of the deal."

"Fuck it. That isn't what I want, baby. It's you."

He gently tips my chin up and strokes my cheek with

his thumb. His eyes glisten in the low lights, they tell me everything I need to know.

This is more than business, more than sex.

This is our future. Our hearts. Our new start in life.

"You're sure? One woman is enough for you?"

I almost want to shake my insecurities away, but they'll never leave me and I have to know.

"You aren't just anyone. You are *my* woman. My wife. You will always be enough."

He sits down on the bed, wrapping a strong arm around my shoulder and I rest my head on his chest.

He picks up the tablet and places it in my hand and my cheeks flush.

"I think the question is, is one man really enough for you?"

I giggle, and he stiffens against me.

Oh shit, he's serious.

"That was once, never again. I only need you." I slide my hands over his abs and cup his growing erection through his pants.

"Well, and him too."

I look up at him and he smirks.

"Keep reading, baby, let me see what gets you going." His deep Russian accent has me squirming in his hold, I do as he says and as I read, he strokes my bare hip.

"Is it good?"

"Hmm?" I lick my lip, in all honesty, I've been more focused on his hardening crotch and the fact his hands are on me. "Pretty decent."

He pushes my device down and I let go of it so it drops to the bed.

Letting out a squeal, he lifts me up and places me on his lap to straddle him. With my arms resting on his shoulders, our noses touching and his fingers digging, almost painfully into my ass.

"Books are there to escape reality, the one I can give you will be everything you could ever dream of. You've had a taste, now let me show you what it would feel like to be mine completely."

My heart races at his words.

"I want you, lastochka. For keeps."

I press my lips against his, the only reaction I can think of right now to show him what he means to me, and then he grips my jaw, pulling me back.

"Say you are mine. Tell me you are my wife, not for business, but for life."

I don't waste a second in my response.

"I'm yours, Roman. Now please make me your good little slut and bend me over until I forget who I am."

"As you wish. But I'll never let you forget our last name."

He pulls back my bottom lip with his thumb. His other hand slides down my sides, sending shivers of anticipation through me.

"How wet is my wife for me?" he whispers against my mouth.

"Soaked."

A sexy smile appears as he dips under my satin panties.

"Hmm," he mutters as he circles my clit lightly, making me pant.

"You passed your first test, now are you ready to play?"

He sinks his fingers inside me and curls them. I tip my head back, letting out a moan.

"I'll take that as a yes, baby." He leans over and begins sucking on my neck.

With his fingers still deep inside of me, I'm flipped over his shoulder and he carries me out of my bedroom.

"Remember, in here, you do exactly as I say. You only come when I allow it. You follow the rules, the pleasure is yours. You don't, you'll be punished accordingly."

"I understand, *sir*."

I bite down on my tongue as he slaps my ass and places me down in the middle of his gigantic bed.

"I need you naked, lastochka," he commands.

Our eyes lock and a darkness flashes across his that only turns me on more.

I quickly get to work, tearing off my cami, shorts and panties. He leans over the bed and swipes them onto the floor.

"On all fours, ass in the air, face on the mattress and arms spread."

I swallow the lump in my throat and get into position.

Nerves wash over me as he tightens the leather strap to my left wrist. I let out a breath as he strokes his fingertip along my arm, all the way down my side and spanks my ass.

Taking my ankle in his hand, I feel the strap go on.

"Look at you, so beautiful. Completely exposed to me and mine. Are you ready to play, Mrs. Petrov?"

He proceeds with my other foot and finishes with my right wrist.

"Y-yes."

A sharp pain radiates from my scalp as he yanks my head up by my hair.

My lips part and he places two fingers there.

"Nice and wet for me," he tells me before sliding them into my mouth to suck.

"Hmm, good girl. I can't wait to have those lips wrapped around my cock."

I nod. Unsure whether to speak.

"Now tell me, Nadia. Do you think you've been good enough to be fucked tonight?"

"I think so."

He tips his head to the side, as if contemplating my answer.

17

ROMAN

SONG, UNDRESS, ROSENFELD

Fuck. I don't think my dick has ever been this hard. Stepping back I look at my wife, strapped to the bed with her ass up in the air, under my full control.

I position myself between her legs, slapping the inside of her thigh before rubbing it and gliding my fingers softly across her glistening pussy.

The moan that escapes her has my cock throbbing.

Taking the little bullet vibrator from my pocket that I snatched without her realizing earlier, I turn it on and the buzzing fills the room. As I tease her entrance she jolts forward, so I grab her by the hips and pull her back to me.

"Stay still, lastochka. You move, I stop. And you're not going to want to miss out on what I have planned for you."

Sliding the vibrator all the way in, I rub my hands over her ass and part her cheeks.

"Oh fuck, Roman," she pants out.

I lick along the inside of her thigh and she shivers under my touch, exactly how I want her. I get to work, sucking on her delicious pussy and switching it to gentle licks that have her shivering.

Her moans grow louder, I pull back and sit on my heels and my hand cracks down on her ass, leaving a growing red mark instantly.

"Shit," she hisses, but she doesn't move.

"Such a perfect little slut, aren't you?"

Taking off my belt and releasing my painfully hard cock, I tease her with the leather, sliding it along the sensitive skin on her back.

She sucks in a breath and squeezes her eyes shut.

"You are owed one punishment, Nadia. You shut down on me. You tried to deny your feelings to me. But, you never left me, did you? You would never leave me, isn't that right? My needy whore wants this."

She nods, sweat beading on her forehead.

Using two fingers, I tease around the vibrator and sink a finger in beside it and fight the groan that comes out of me as she stretches around me.

I keep the belt rubbing her skin and feel her wetness drip down to my wrist.

"Oh, you want to be punished, don't you?"

I bite back my grin. She is perfect for me.

"Y-yes. Roman," she says breathlessly.

Her walls clench around my finger. She's close. I want her to shatter around me. Removing my hand, in one swift motion, she screams out as I hold her in place by the hip and crack the belt across her ass.

Before she has time to process the pain, I pull out the slim vibrator and press it against her asshole.

Her cries turn into perfect moans, and my name leaving her lips in pure ecstasy is enough for me.

So I sink my cock deep inside that tight pussy, keeping the vibrator on her ass, but not putting it in.

I start with slow movements, pushing down on the top

of her back so I can hit the spot inside that has her almost convulsing.

"You feel so good, lastochka. Fuck."

Her nails dig into the comforter as I slam in and out of her, pushing the vibrator in her ass just a touch.

As she squishes her face into the mattress, I wrap her hair around my fist, yanking her back up to ride her.

"Do you want to come, baby?"

She nods and I pull myself all the way out to the tip, at the same time sinking the vibrator in a tiny bit more. Her lips part, she's falling apart around me, yet keeping her orgasm at bay.

"You're doing such a good job, Nadia. Being so good for me." I praise her, and the flush on her neck deepens in color.

I pound into her, all the way to the base, pulling at her hair as I do.

"Oh my god," she moans.

Her legs begin to shake, so I start to fuck her with everything I have, bringing myself closer to the tipping point. All I can focus on is how good it feels to fuck my wife.

The room is filled with the sounds of our moans, I slap her ass one more time.

"I-I need to—"

"Come for me." I cut her off with an order.

She sucks in a breath, I pull her head back further. She's fought herself not to come for this long, she needs something to push her.

"Come. For. Me. No fighting it. Be a good girl. Give it to me."

I keep thrusting into her, pushing the vibrator all the way in her ass and she explodes around me.

I ride her through her climax, reaching my own as her tight cunt strangles my cock and I fill her up. Her name is on my lips as I tip my head back and finish, with probably the most aggressive orgasm I've had.

I keep pumping her slowly, easing out the toy in her ass and try to regain my own breath. Letting go of her hair, her head slumps against the mattress and I start to massage her back, I don't want to pull out of her yet.

So I keep rubbing circles over her and down to her perfectly red ass.

"Ugh, that feels so good," she says with a lazy smile on her lips.

"I'll remember that."

Reluctantly, I pull out of her, admiring how my cum spills down the inside of her thighs.

I quickly get to work releasing her from her binds and lift her spent body against me, pressing a kiss on her temple.

"You are such a good girl," I whisper and she grins at me.

"Thank you, Roman," she says, her voice all croaky.

"Anything for you, baby."

After cleaning her up in the en-suite, she's back in my arms again and I get beneath the covers beside her, pulling her into a cuddle.

Never have I done this. But, this isn't just any woman or a sub. This is my wife. The love of my life.

"This bed is divine, Rom," she says sleepily, snuggling into my bare chest, making small circles with her nail.

"My wife will sleep in here with me from now on."

She looks up at me through her thick lashes and smiles, revealing her perfectly white teeth.

"No objections from me. As long as you're the big spoon."

I roll her onto her side, pressing against her and I grab her breast in my hand, pinching her nipple so she yelps.

"Well, you best be prepared to wake up with my cock poking you in the ass, it will be up to you to rectify the situation."

"Every morning?"

"Problem?" I say, lightly biting her bare shoulder.

"Nope, as long as I get the same treatment back." She wiggles against me and fuck, my dick is already standing to attention.

"I told you, I'll give you everything, baby. Now sleep."

Kissing the back of her head, I let my eyes close and focus on her breathing against me.

This feels too good to ever let go.

This is my life. She is my life.

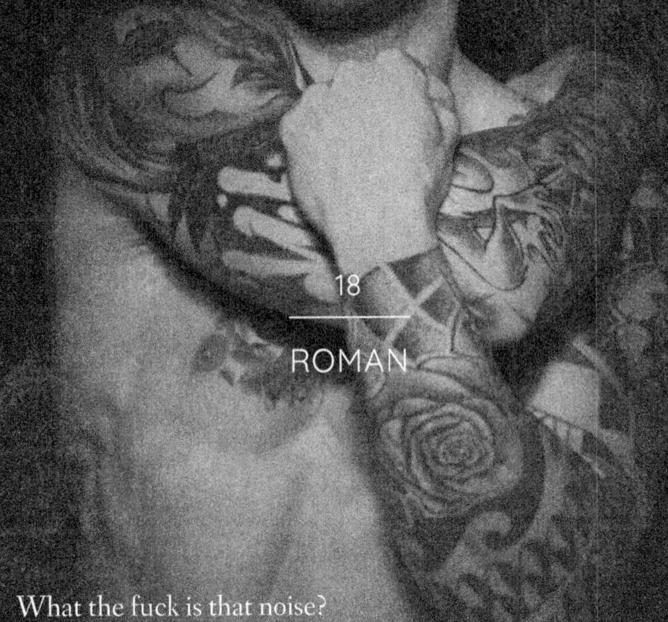

18

ROMAN

What the fuck is that noise?

I don't want to move. I just want to lay here with my arms wrapped around my naked wife.

She murmurs in her sleep and shifts, pressing herself tighter against me.

Her soft curves touch me in all the right places making my cock swell between her ass cheeks.

I'm half tempted to wake her up by plunging into her pussy that's still dripping with my cum.

But that sound hits again.

Damn it. It's my phone.

"What?" I croak. It has to be something like three in the morning.

Entirely too late for bullshit.

"Mr. Petrov?" Violet's shaky voice comes through. "We have alarms going off at the Empire. Did you want me to call the police?"

With a groan, I roll away from Nadia's hot body and run my hand down my face. I don't want the cops anywhere near that place.

They'd start asking questions about all of the surveillance cameras I'm having installed, and the secret hallways for high end clients.

"No. What about sending Marco and Rico over?" That's why I hired them. Muscle.

"They're currently working on removing a loud crowd of football players." She has a tinge of desperation behind her words.

"Fine. I'll take care of it." I hit the button to end the call and slide out of the covers.

The air conditioning keeps it cool enough at night to make my dick twinge when it hits the air.

I should be back soon, I'll wake Nadia up to warm myself.

Dressing quickly, I rush down the stairs and into my car.

The parking lot is quiet, and empty, when I pull in. Heat radiates from the cracked asphalt when I step out.

Grabbing my gun and my flashlight, I work my way slowly towards the main entrance.

I don't see any signs of broken glass, so I check the alarm on my app.

Yep, something is still triggering it inside the building.

Shit.

I hit the code to unlock the door, and wait for it to close silently behind me.

The darkness absorbs the sounds, and the smell of paint and sheetrock hang heavy in the air.

My ears strain to hear any noise, but nothing moves.

Creeping quietly over the array of extension cords strewn across the floor, I start working my way slowly to the first room.

The glow of the flashlight highlights the aim of the barrel of my pistol.

Nothing.

Another corner to an empty hall.

I wish I knew the layout in here better. I've barely spent any time, but have indulged in every free minute with Nadia instead.

I'd rather know every inch of her body than this place.

It doesn't have the same appeal.

Huh. My priorities seem to have shifted.

There's a piece of my mind telling me to say "fuck it" and leave. Let whatever criminal do their deed, I'll clean up the mess later.

Whoever they are, they can have the place. I got what I needed out of the deal.

I'm nearly halfway into the building when I decide I'm done. It's been almost two hours. I haven't found any sign, and I'm tired of wasting my time.

Something crunches under my foot.

Broken glass?

With a burst of pain, my weapon and light fall from my hands as a crowbar is slammed over my arms from a hidden door.

Rolling backwards, I duck and narrowly avoid a crashing blow towards my head.

Fuck.

My wrist screams at me when I push myself up and scramble backwards.

"I was hoping it would be you." A menacing voice echoes through the dark corridor.

Shadows of a man loom over me, and he kicks my gun away with a rattle.

"Do you have any idea how much money it cost me to hire those men to keep your goons busy? I didn't think you'd want the cops here." When a flicker of illumination hits, I recognize the hollow eyes of that asshole Drew Allen.

"Of course it's you," I grunt, holding my left arm against my body. It feels like it might be broken.

Hurts like a bitch. "I didn't make your wife cheat on you, dipshit. She came to the club all on her own."

He swings his weapon like a bat, making me jump out of his reach.

"She wouldn't have been there if you didn't exist!" His voice cracks and he lunges towards me, the sharp tines aiming for my gut.

"You're insane, you know that?" Or, maybe I'm the crazy one, trying to yell at the man with the death wish, while I don't have anything to defend myself.

Turning, I run in the direction of the exit.

But, the hook of the crowbar snags around my ankle, sending me hurdling onto my chest on the cold floor.

This guy is pissing me off.

My foot shoots out, catching him in the side of the knee.

With a cry, he topples over, and I hear the heavy steel bar bounce off of the concrete.

I kick out again, trying to connect with his head, but my heel glances across his shoulder. My hand doesn't want to hold my weight, so I use my elbow to push myself up.

His shoes scrape, and I can hear him chasing me around the corner.

This isn't going to end well for one of us.

And, I don't lose. Nadia being naked in my bed proves that.

Making a hard turn, I grab the frame to pull myself into the next dark room.

The smell of chemicals makes my nose burn. Holding my breath, I wait for his footsteps.

As he tries to run past, I fling the door open.

The thump when he hits it echoes through the empty building, followed by a grunt as he falls again.

A metal cylinder tips and rolls against the wall when I shift.

This is exactly what I need.

Grabbing the end, I flip it over and charge out into the hall and raise it over my head.

Swinging it as hard as I can, I connect with the middle of his back.

The high pitch scream reverbates off of the paneled walls making my ears buzz.

I drop my arm again, this time he deflects the blow with his elbow.

Hooking my calf, he jerks my leg out from under me, and the back of my skull hits hard enough to make stars shoot in front of my eyes.

Fuck.

His fingers dig into my thigh, then my ribs as he straddles me.

The first fist finds my cheek. Another hits me in the temple making the ringing in my head even worse.

No way am I going out like this.

Flipping the metal tube, I find the aperture on the end, and pull the trigger to kick out a blast of a blue flame into his eyes.

Both of his hands jerk to his face, but I don't let go.

Fire catches into his hair, and heavy shirt.

Leaping off of me, he backpedals through into the room I was hiding in.

Shit.

I know those smells that are in there.

Dragging myself as quickly as I can, I manage to get just

past a flimsy wall when it feels like all of the air is sucked out of my lungs.

God damn it, no!

I'm dizzy as hell, but I push myself to my feet and try to run.

A ball of flame whooshes around me and knocks me back to the tile.

His scream reaches new highs until the blaze silences him.

I have to get out.

The plume of toxic smoke boils over me, choking me with the fumes.

Trying to cover my nose and breathe through my sleeve, I keep crawling towards the entrance.

My eyes burn, and darkness absorbs the haze, making it almost impossible for me to tell which way I have to go.

Coughing, I slump to my belly and try to pull myself further.

I'm so dizzy, I can't focus.

Maybe, if I just lay down for a moment, the air will clear.

19

NADIA

I'm not sure what startles me awake.

But, the bed is cold where Roman is supposed to be.

Where is he?

Finding my robe, I find myself moving to the kitchen.

Usually, he's up and has coffee made before I get here. The machine is empty and dry.

What the heck?

It takes me a little while to track down my phone, and when I do, it's showing three missed calls from an unknown number.

Two of those, they left a message.

"This is for Mrs. Nadia Petrov. Your husband is currently at General Medical, but is being transferred soon. Please contact us as soon as possible." It's a woman's voice, and she sounds genuinely irritated in the second recording.

A cold sweat covers my body and a chill works down my spine.

Hospital?

He's hurt?

I hit redial, and pace until someone picks up.

It only takes three people transferring me before I hear the same sounding person from the messages on the other end.

"Oh, yes. Mrs. Petrov, your husband is actually being transferred right now." Her nasally tone is starting to grate on my nerves.

"Where? What happened? Is he okay?" I'm frantic to get some answers.

"He was involved in a building fire and has suffered some smoke inhalation. He's being transferred to the Las Vegas Jail for processing." She clips her words, like she's trying to hurry.

"Wait, jail? Why?" My head is spinning.

He was just here, now he's being locked up?

"I don't have that information, you'll have to call their office to find out more." The line goes quiet.

That bitch just hung up on me after dropping that kind of news?

In a flurry, I grab clothes, my purse, my phone, and anything else I can think of.

How did this all happen?

My fingers fly over the search function as I climb in my car.

I don't even know where I'm going, but I have to go somewhere.

"Rochelle? I need help." I can count on her.

"Tell me." There's a clanging noise in the background and a shuffle.

I bet she's dropped her scissors and is already running towards the door.

She's the kind of friend that everyone needs. No questions.

"They took him to jail." The tears start to sting as the reality sets in.

"Oh, no. Don't worry. I got you. Meet me there." Her keys jingle.

I wonder if she remembered to lock up.

No, I really don't care.

"I don't know where I'm going," I sob. The street signs blur through my welling eyes.

"Where are you? Park. I'll get you." Her determination pushes through my anxiety and calms me enough to focus around me.

"Um. There's the parking lot next to the Cornpot Cafe." That should be easy enough for her to find.

I've hardly switched the vehicle to park before I lose it over my steering wheel.

The man I never thought I'd like, I suddenly feel like I can't be without.

How badly is he hurt? Will they find out about Vlad?

Oh my god, do they know already?

A rapid knock on the window has me looking up to find Rochelle pounding on my door.

"Come on, let's go." Her bracelets rattle as she clutches me around my shoulders in a fast hug.

Pushing her broad glasses up over her nose, she settles me into the passenger seat before prancing around the hood in her six inch heels.

She makes it look graceful in a hurry.

But, when she sits down, she quickly digs her inhaler out of her leather purse. "All this excitement has kicked up my asthma." She expertly spins us out of the lot while puffing away.

I find myself clinging to her arm as we take the steps leading into the concrete building.

A surly, squat officer sits behind a bullet proof glass window. His squinty eyes don't even move when we approach him.

"Um. Excuse me? I'm looking for my husband." It feels strange to say it, but also, somehow, right.

His thick neck wrinkles as he turns his head. "'Kay? What's his name?"

"Roman Petrov."

His face turns a mottled shade of red. "I'll have him sent down. You need to go through that door—" He points a fat finger at a heavy steel barricade. "—and the guard in there will set you up."

Rochelle leans close to me once we're far enough. "You know this isn't normal. Usually there's no visiting until after arraignment. Your man must be special."

"He is," I whisper.

The thin man in here points me to a cold chair facing a thick plexiglass window with a phone.

It isn't long before Roman is led in, chains hanging from his wrists and ankles.

His orange jumpsuit hangs off of him, and his sleeves are rolled up, exposing his tattooed forearms.

He normally has his dark hair slicked back, but it's loose and curls down over his forehead.

I didn't expect him to look so damn sexy in here. But, he's behind a wall that I can't touch him through. And, there's no telling when I'll be able to hold him again.

I almost start crying all over again.

"Hey, baby." He smiles at me from the other side of the clear wall as he talks to me through the earpiece. "I'm glad you came to see me."

"What happened? Why are you here?" I can't stop my voice from cracking.

He glances at the men standing near him. “The alarms went off at the Empire. I went in to check it out. Then a fire broke out.”

Looking closer, I can see the singed hairs on the top of his head, and bruises around his eyes.

“What are they charging you with?” I say quietly.

He sighs, sitting back as far as the short cord will let him. “Arson and murder.”

My fingers fly to my lips. “Oh, Roman. Is it—”

He cuts me off with a wave of his hand. “There was a guy there, he broke in.”

“That’s so scary. I’m glad you’re okay.” My palm presses against the window dividing us.

My father’s club, gone. Strangely, it doesn’t bother me.

“Hey. I see the worry knotting up that pretty brow.” His hand covers mine on the other side. “I’ll be out of here soon.”

“What can I do?” I just got him, I’m not ready to let go.

“You keep that tight little pussy wet for me in my bed, baby. I’m gonna victory fuck you when I get home,” he says confidently.

I chew on my lip. “But, what if you don’t win?”

A smirk lifts his lip. “I don’t lose.”

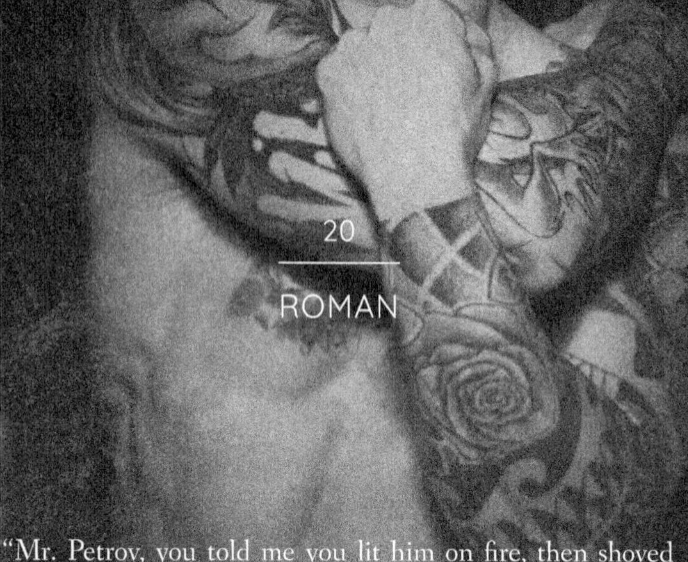

20

ROMAN

"Mr. Petrov, you told me you lit him on fire, then shoved him into a room filled with accelerants. I really think you should think about changing your plea to 'guilty'. If you go in front of a jury, they'll string you up to the fullest extent." My lawyer wipes the sweat from his wide forehead with a crisp white handkerchief.

"What ended up happening to the Empire?" I'm not even mad it is delayed in opening.

He wrings his hands before answering. "It's a total loss."

"Tommy, how long have you worked for me?" I narrow my eyes and watch him dart his gaze from me to the door.

"Four years," he stammers.

I lean forward, my handcuffs clink against the metal table. "And, in that time, how many thousands of hours of footage have we accumulated?

"P-Probably millions."

"And, how many yachts have I bought you so you can take my girls out onto the lake with you?" My fingers weave together.

I might find someone new after this one.

"This is my second, after my first one sunk." His cheeks pale.

I think he knows where I'm going with this.

"Because you overdosed that hooker with shit cocaine, so I helped you cover it up?"

His hand shakes as he drags the damp cloth over his face. "Yes, boss. You did."

"If you don't want that mess bobbing back to the surface, you tell the judge exactly what I say. Understand?" I'm firing him after today.

His chin wobbles as he nods furiously.

"Good. Let's go." Kicking back my chair, I wave through the window to the guard stationed outside.

The stoic officer and two of his pals lead us to the main courtroom.

After all the oaths, the grizzled judge looks down at me with his bushy eyebrows furrowed. "Mr. Roman Petrov. How do you plead?"

I elbow Tommy.

"He pleads not-guilty, your honor," he sounds much more confident than he did a few moments ago.

Funny how a solid threat can firm up someone's resolve.

Judge Collins leans back, his lips pursing under his gray mustache. "And does the defendant have anything to say?"

Tommy shifts next to me. He knows as well as I do, this isn't the normal protocol.

"Yes, your honor. February eighteenth, three years ago." My hands clasp in front of me in a relaxed pose as I wait.

First one fat eyebrow, then the other raise and drop.

Then, the lips flatten and the furrows along his nose deepen as a frown takes shape.

There it is.

His little brain is racing, connecting the dots.

Running through all the possible scenarios of what I could possibly mean by what I said.

Even Tommy looks at me quizzically from my side.

I don't budge. I just watch the old man on the podium.

He's the modicum of justice, truth, and righteousness.

But, I know better.

I have his secrets on a hard drive, with back ups.

And a fleet of people who will open those up to be loosed upon the world at a single word from me.

"Roman," Tommy whispers.

I squint at him without looking.

It should be any moment now.

The judge's age-speckled hand shakes as he raises his gavel and drops it with a sharp rap.

"Case dismissed."

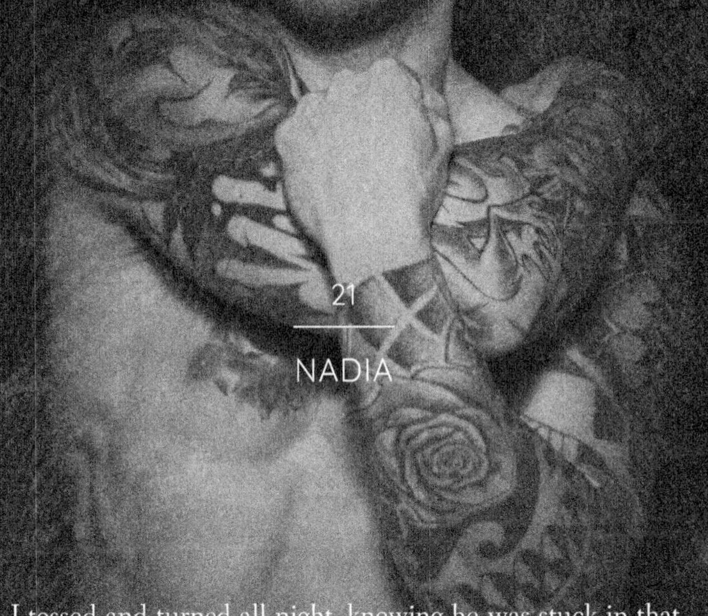

21

NADIA

I tossed and turned all night, knowing he was stuck in that cold jail cell makes me miserable.

It hurts that I'm finally here, in his bed, without him.

The irony doesn't miss me. I found a man who lets me become the person I always knew I could be. He unlocked the pieces that I'd hidden, even from myself.

And now, he's gone.

The worst part, I wasn't allowed to attend his arraignment. No one would tell me what happened. There's no information online.

Just, silence.

Rochelle was able to stay late, but she's back at the workshop getting ready.

Maybe that's where I should be. Being busy will make the time go faster.

But, for how long?

Murder carries a huge sentence. He could go away for years, or even *decades*.

Oh, God. That would be awful.

I should be thankful he wanted to take care of me, and

set me up with a substantial bank account. If my big show goes well, between the sales and the money he's set aside for me, I should stay comfortable.

I'd give it all up to have him back.

That feeling he gives me, like I'm the most important person in the room, as if his entire world revolves around me, I'd rather have that.

Because I feel the same way about him.

One coffee isn't enough to lift this melancholy from my bones. Exhaustion of the heart is caffeine proof.

Maybe another will perk me up enough that I at least have the energy to work on the last dress for my fashion line.

I'm just sliding the decanter back into place when a large pair of hands wrap around my waist and turn me around.

"Roman!" Flinging myself around his neck, he lifts me easily to sit on the kitchen counter.

"Did you miss me?" His hot breath fans over my neck as his dark eyes bore into me.

"Nope. Not even a little. It's been very peaceful here." I fight the grin trying to overtake my mouth.

His palms circle my throat and he tips my chin up with his thumbs. "Stop being a brat," he growls. "If you want a spanking, just ask. Now, did you miss your husband?"

My smile fades as the truth makes my chin tremble. "Why? You know I did. I've been worried sick."

His hips work between my knees as he moves closer. "Why? Because all I could focus on was getting back to you. Nothing else even entered my mind. Just you. Which tells me something—"

"Tells you what?" I cut him off.

"That I'm fucking madly in love with you to the point of

delusion. The only single thing that matters to me is you, my wife. I want to spend the rest of my days showing you what it's like to be loved by me. For real. No business, just love." He ducks his head, meeting my lips with his in a ferocious kiss.

Breathlessly, I pull back. He loves me? "What about the club? I heard on the news it burned to the ground."

His dark hair falls over his eyes as he shakes his head. "It doesn't mean anything to me if I don't have you by my side, lastochka."

"But, I thought you wanted that more than anything?" My nails dig into his back and my knees quiver in worry that he won't want me any more.

His fingers thread through my hair and he tilts my face up so our noses almost touch.

"Priorities change. That life, I don't need it. I have enough money for us to last a lifetime. We can do whatever the hell we want. I wanted that club because I couldn't have it. Out of greed. My purpose was building an empire. Now, I want that with you, baby." He strokes my cheek and his lips follow his strokes.

I search his eyes. There's a moment where I feel like I need to hold back. But, I want this with him. The need to feel complete outweighs the last of my reservations. "I don't want to have anything to do with that establishment. After seeing what it did to my dad. It ruined him, and our family. I don't want that for...ours."

"Consider them gone. Why do I need them when my wife is such a good girl for me, hmm?" His hands grip beneath my thighs and he hoists me around his waist. "I've been in jail for four days, and all I could think about is how much I missed you. And, how little I cared about everything else."

He carries me into the living room, and sprawls me onto the couch beneath him.

"Did you really? I was worried you'd be locked up forever." The weight of him over me makes my pussy pulse.

"And if I was? Would you have waited for me?" His lips find my neck and he sucks his way down towards my collar.

"Yes," I pant. It's getting harder to focus on his words as his mouth moves lower.

"Tell me why you'd wait." He folds my shirt away from my body and runs his hand into my leggings.

"Because—" I trail off. Am I ready to admit it to myself?

His teeth bite down on my exposed nipple. "You're asking for a spanking." He leans back and strips his belt from his pants. "Tell me," he demands.

"Because I love you," I scream as his fingers plunge inside me.

"How much?" He presses, twisting his wrist, holding me in place by my neck.

"Fuck. All of it. Every single bit."

His lips slam over mine as he works me to a state of bliss, my hips grind against his hand to match his rhythm.

"Hmm, so needy for me."

I feel empty when he withdraws, with a mischievous glint in his eyes, he puts his fingers against my lips.

"The taste of love is sweet, isn't it?" He pushes them inside my mouth and I suck them clean.

"God, I love you." He whispers against my cheek, moving lower with his tongue down the column of my neck and sucking on my flesh. My back arches, pressing my breasts against him.

His fingers slide out of my mouth with a pop, with the lightest of touches he traces them over my nipple, before taking it between the two and pinching.

"More," I pant out.

"I said I'd give you everything, I intend to start by having you sit on my face."

I don't know how he lifts me so effortlessly, but within seconds I am flipped around, he's on his back and I'm perched over him.

"Now this is where a wife should sit, on her husband's face."

I let out a giggle, but then as his tongue swipes across my needy pussy, my head tips back. His fingers painfully dig into my hips as he pushes me down, completely smothering him so he can devour me.

And like every moment I am with Roman, my mind stops swirling. I am free. I am exactly who I am meant to be with him.

And that makes me come so much harder than I ever have in my life.

MY LIFE HAS CHANGED SO MUCH since I began to get ready for this show.

In the last few weeks, I've lost my father, gained and lost a club, but won the best prize of all.

My loving husband.

Who knew that the man with the darkest reputation could become the shining light in my heart?

"Are you ready for this? We're about to rock Vegas, baby!" Rochelle clings briefly to my arm before she scurries to follow one of the models. "Kanesha, girl! We need to fix that sleeve! Wait for me, I have short legs!" Her heels click over the marble tiles towards the dressing room.

It's surreal, seeing the ideas I had in my head become

reality. Silks and chiffons adorn the gorgeous women and men who've been hired to wear my designs.

"None as beautiful as you." Roman's hand clasps my waist and he pulls me tightly to his body before placing a gentle kiss on my temple.

"What?" I have so many things going through my mind, I'm not really sure where he's coming from.

"I see that look on your face. The little furrow you get between your eyes when you think you aren't good enough." His warm thumb finds the spot above my nose and he rubs gently. "I can assure you, no one in this room glows as brightly as you."

A warm feeling spreads through me.

I love how he knows my fears and calms me.

But, when the announcers gets on the loudspeaker to begin the event, my stomach lurches and my pulse skyrockets.

"I'll be just outside if you need me, in the best seat in the house." He squeezes my ass before he leaves.

He'll be right in the center, impossible to miss.

My biggest cheerleader.

Clapping my hands, I draw everyone's attention backstage. "Okay everyone! It's a really big night! Elizabeth Devonson is here tonight. Let's put on a good show for her!"

Wide eyes and frantic claps run through the models before they scurry to their places.

Roman's deep pockets have helped with hiring the best makeup artists and helpers. I just hope it's enough to catch Elizabeth's eye.

As the music starts, the happy murmuring from the audience is enough to lighten my worries.

They really like them!

I can see Elizabeth smiling and pointing from where I hide behind the curtain.

"Did she see the Brazilian patterns? How about the Monaco inspired one?" Rochelle hangs on my arm between her manic circles through the wardrobes. "What does she think?" she asks anxiously.

"I don't know. She's smiling. That's good, right?" My doubts try to press down on me, but I still have one more outfit to send out.

The one inspired by Roman. Him sneaking a peek at my sketchbook, then showing me his tattoos, was enough to send my ideas whirling.

A heavily brocade suit, lined with iridescent threads that highlight the seams to almost glimmer in the lights. They lightly mimic the swirls and lines of his ink, but almost dance with movement as the model strides down the runway.

It only would have looked better if it was on the broad shoulders of my man. His imposing presence would really bring home the full effect of what I want.

There's a collective gasp from the gathering.

Are they standing?

Applause rattles the windows, and the cheers are so loud my ears ring.

The man wearing my suit has barely exited the stage when a rush of bodies flow from the seating area to surround me.

Elizabeth is in the front.

"I absolutely must have that suit!" she squeals as she pulls me in for a hug.

"My-my last outfit?" I didn't think it would be the star. I made that as a way to exhibit my love for Roman, to show the world that he's my knight.

"Yes, darling. Please, let me showcase it!" She brushes her wild hair back from her shoulders in an extravagant gesture. "You're going to be famous!"

A hand lands on my lower back, and Roman's lips move close to my ear. "I knew you'd do amazing."

"Miss! Miss!" There's a lanky man behind Elizabeth. His calls make Roman's fingers tighten on my hip.

"It's "Mrs.Petrov"." Roman corrects him with a growl.

The thin guy's face pales and he nods emphatically. "I'm sorry, yes. I'm Parker Glass, I work for Entwersh."

My heart feels like it stops.

"No way," I whisper.

Roman tilts his head, but doesn't ask.

"Whatever Elizabeth offers for that suit, I'll double it." Two of his boney fingers rise.

"What? You've got to be kidding me!" Elizabeth scoffs. "I knew her first!"

This must be a dream.

The clicks of Rochelle's heels get closer and she grabs my free arm. "Nadia! It went so well!" She grows quiet when she sees Elizabeth's red face. "What is going on?" she mouths.

"Bidding war." I can hardly contain my excitement. It's a struggle to keep my expression neutral.

Rochelle's nails dig into my elbow, and I can feel her vibrating next to me.

Elizabeth's eyes narrow, but then a slow smile spreads over her face. "I'm going to max you out, Parker. Then I'm buying the rest of her line."

My god.

A low squeal begins to come out of Rochelle.

This is a life changer, especially for her. She won't have to worry about her medical bills ever again.

Roman steps between us, raising his hands. "We'll sit down next week and work out the details. I'm sure everyone can come to a happy agreement."

"Are you her manager?" Parker pipes up.

"Better. I'm her husband." Roman turns and wraps his arm around me, then leads us away with Rochelle following.

"I knew you could do it, baby." He squeezes my hand and pulls it up to kiss my fingers. "You're magic."

"I couldn't have done it without you, Rom. I know you put in a word for me with Elizabeth those weeks ago." There's no way she would have known who I was.

"Are you mad I pulled some strings? All she had to do was see you. No one is making them buy your designs. That's all you and your talent." The love is obvious in his gaze.

"I'm not angry. I'm thankful that you cared enough to try and help." My ex would have never done that. He thought my interest in fashion was just a hobby and never took it seriously.

I needed a real man to respect me enough to be supportive.

Once we're safely backstage and away from the crowds, Rochelle stops and screams. "I can't freaking believe that!"

Erupting into giggles, we clutch each other, shrieking in laughter and tears.

All of our hard work, the stress, the planning. It all paid off tonight.

Dreams really do come true.

22

ROMAN

ALKALINE, SLEEP TOKEN

With the biggest bunch of deep pink roses I could get my hands on, on my way home, I close the door quietly behind me.

I want to surprise Nadia.

Her show was a huge success, and even though we spent all night celebrating in the bedroom, I wanted to do something for her tonight.

As I make my way through the hall, expecting to find her relaxing on the couch, I frown when she isn't there.

"Nadia, baby?" I call out.

"Out here, Rom." Her sweet voice brings me peace, yet also makes my cock twitch instantly thinking about what I've done to her.

And what I plan to do to her after our date tonight.

I slide open the door to the patio. She has her feet up on the table and a glass of red wine. She bends forward, as she does I can see her pink thong poking out from her shorts and I hold back my groan.

Picking up the empty glass on the table, she pours it and

hands it to me. As soon as she spots the flowers in my hand her face lights up and my heart almost skips a beat.

"For you, lastochka."

Leaning down, I press my lips against hers.

"They're so pretty," she gushes. "They are the same color as my dress last night." Her cheeks flush as she takes the flowers and presses them to her nose to take a long inhale.

"I'm not just a pretty face." I wink at her.

She giggles, setting them down on the table. I pour myself a drink from the bottle and sit beside her, wrapping my arm over her shoulders and pulling her against me.

"Good day at work?" she asks, resting her head on my chest as I stroke her smooth skin.

"It was okay, the contractors have a plan for The Empire, we should be up and running soon."

She stiffens against me.

There won't be any doubts in her mind in a few minutes.

"That's good."

"You're lying. Do you want to be punished?" I grab her ponytail and tip her head back so she can see how serious I am.

I press my nose against hers.

"If you want to come in the next week, don't hide what you're really thinking."

"You'd really not let me come for a whole week?"

There is panic in her eyes and I chuckle.

"Yes. Seven full days. No orgasms."

She shakes her head and bites her lip.

"So, tell me the truth."

She tries to lower her chin but I hold my grip in her hair firm.

"The club. I still don't want it. It brings up too many memories of my dad. I'm kinda glad it burned down. But, I also need the money to pay off the damn debts and keep my company running."

I scrunch my brows.

"No. You don't. You're my wife. Money isn't a problem for us. In fact..."

I pull out our original contract and the divorce packet from my pocket, releasing her hair. She looks at me with confusion, that damn pout of hers turning me on.

"Our original deal is meaningless now. You have half an empire, this marriage is a real marriage. I don't want it to end. We build your company together. We do whatever the hell we want with the building, together. There is no stipulation we have to run it as it was."

My brain trails off with what could be one of the best ideas I've ever had.

"What if we close it as a club and make it into a full workshop for you? We can build off a secret play area that's just for us. Whatever we want to explore, perhaps for date nights?"

"You'd really lose a club for me?"

I nod. No question.

"I like the idea of a playroom." I smirk at her and watch the crimson spreads up her neck. It makes me wrap my fingers around her throat and pull her lips to mine. "A place where I can steal you away, spank that perfect ass, and make you scream my name over and over? That sounds like the ideal workplace. Just for us."

Placing the contracts on her lap, I pull away and search her eyes, filled with love.

"Tear it up," I demand.

"You're sure? You really don't want the divorce?" Her voice shakes.

"Do I seem like a man who doesn't know what he wants?" I tip my head to the side.

"No. Not at all," she chuckles, picking up the paper.

Her dark eyes don't leave mine as she tears right down the center of the pages, the ripping filling the air.

The end of our beginning and making way for something much better. A real marriage, no deal, no club.

Just love.

"Good girl."

Picking up the torn papers from her lap, I look down at the fractured words. I never want to see this again in my life. Taking out the lighter from my inside pocket, I flick it and let the flame catch the corner of the first half and toss it in the fire pit beside me, repeating the process with the other half.

I turn to Nadia, who is watching me with amusement.

"Really want that gone don't you? You must really love me." She licks her lip and I grab her cheeks.

"You have no idea. It's more than a want, it's an all consuming fire within me."

Her soft hand strokes my jaw.

"I like that."

"Well, I love you."

Pushing myself back, I do what I intended to do when I stepped through the door.

I sink down onto one knee and retrieve the brand new sparkling diamond ring from my jacket and open up the box for her.

A huge gem, surrounded by smaller ones, glimmers in the patio lights. The price of this is more than the whole damn club.

It's worth it.

"Roman," she gushes, her hands covering her mouth.

"I wanted to get you a ring that means something, bought out of love, not obligation. Something to show you how special you are to me."

"You didn't need to do all of this, I'm never going anywhere. I'm proud to be your wife." She leans in closer, brushing her full lips along the shell of my ear.

"And being a good girl just for you," she whispers.

Fuck. This woman is divine. Complete perfection. And all mine.

She holds out her hand and splays her fingers to let me push the gold band over her knuckle.

"It's so beautiful." Her eyes twinkle from the reflections, like stars in the night sky.

Without wasting a second, I push open her thighs. I'm already on my knees for her, I might as well make myself useful and fuck her with my tongue. Show her what a good husband she has.

"Shorts and panties, gone."

Her lips make an "O" but she doesn't hesitate, she lifts her hips and pulls her clothes down, spreading her legs, leaving me salivating as I look at her soaking cunt.

"Such a pretty pussy, so desperate for me, isn't it?"

I trace a finger along the inside of her thigh, relishing the effect I have over her. A simple touch sends her crazy. Her pupils dilate, her skin flushes, her breathing becomes heavier, all from a simple stroke.

"P-please."

"Is this what you want?" I follow my tongue behind the path of my finger.

"Sir, yes please."

"Oh, I love it when you beg, lastochka. For that, I'll give you what you need."

I reward her with circles on her clit. Her little moans are fueling me.

I want to drag this out, bring her to the edge over and over on my tongue until she has no choice but to fuck my face and take what she needs.

I have all the time in the world for her pretty pussy.

"More?" I ask as her hips roll. "I'll take that as a yes."

Sliding two fingers inside her, I get to work, sucking and licking until she's clamping around me and gripping onto my hair hard enough for it to sting my scalp.

"Not yet, baby. I haven't had my fill."

Even though my dick is aching to pound into her, I push one of her knees back so it's to her chest, meaning I can sink my fingers in deeper and curl them to hit her g-spot.

Fuck. She's soaking my face and I'm licking up every single drop.

"I can't hold it. Roman. Please. Let me-“”

I look up at her coming apart, barely holding herself together. Her eyes meet mine, wild and full of hunger. For me.

Twisting my finger, I suck on her clit and she bites her lips shut and squeezes her eyes closed.

"Be a good slut and come all over my face."

Her screams fill my ears, a beautiful sound that almost has me joining her in my pants.

Licking her clean as she rides her orgasm out on my tongue, watching every second she shatters around me, I've never seen such a stunning sight.

I don't let her fully come down before I replace my fingers and release my cock, lining it up with her entrance, using the backrest of the chair to hold myself over her.

She grabs onto the lapels of my suit and tugs me closer.

"Kiss me and make love to me."

I have never done that before, and right now there is nothing else I want to do more.

So I sink in, inch by inch, kissing her softly until she's full. Her legs wrap around my waist and she holds me in place.

"I love you, Roman Petrov. I love you so damn much."

Taking my weight with one hand, I caress her face.

"The only thing that matters to me, now and for the rest of my life, is you. I love you, Nadia."

Her head rolls back, and she looks at me through heavy lids. "Fuck, you feel so good inside me."

Jesus.

Resting more forehead against her, with slow strokes I make love to my wife.

Pure fucking heaven.

"I'm going to come so hard and fill you up, maybe even make a baby."

Her eyes flutter open. "Shit, that's hot. Do it."

Her lips crash over mine, and she moans into my mouth as we both reach our peak.

"I love you," I grit out as I spill into her.

Her body starts to shake and she breaks with me.

"I love you, too."

She gives me a shy smile and I can't help but kiss her.

"Again?" she asks.

"We have time for another round. But then we have somewhere to be..."

This could be interesting to say the least. But this woman is important to me and my family needs to meet the woman who changed the course of my life.

"Where?" She raises an eyebrow.

"My father's. To meet my family."

"That sounds... fun."

I nod.

"We can make it fun. Then, we come home and build the life the women in your books would be jealous of."

THE END

23

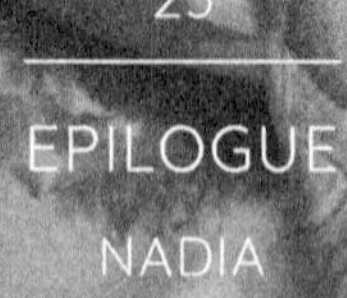

EPILOGUE

NADIA

Just as the front door opens to his father's home, I jump and bite back the gasp as my vibrator buzzes to life inside of me. Roman's hand tightens on my hip, but I can't even look at him.

My cheeks are burning as his dad introduces himself.

Can he hear this? I swear I can hear the buzzing.

"Dad, this is my wife, Nadia." Roman has a look of pride as he rests his palm on the small of my back.

"Umm, hi, Mr. Petrov. So lovely to meet you." I extend out my hand to the gray-bearded man. Tattoos poke from his sleeve, and his dark eyes crinkle in the corners with a smile. I can see the resemblance.

Handsome runs strong in their genes.

He grins, looking between his son and me.

"Call me Nikolai."

I suck in a breath as the vibrations get more intense, and begin pulsing inside me. Squeezing my thighs together only makes it worse when it hits that spot on my clit.

"You're doing so well keeping yourself composed, baby," Roman whispers against my ear.

"Son, good to see you." He pulls Roman in for a hug.

Sweeping his arm away, he invites a red haired woman who's younger than me to move into his side. "Roman, this is my wife Natalia." He turns to the green eyed beauty. She's noticeably pregnant, and looks radiant.

My husband reaches forward and takes her hand politely. "Welcome to this insane family, Natalia."

She blushes, and it matches her hair. "Thank you. It's nice to meet everyone. Nikolai is happy you made it, we were worried you wouldn't."

I straighten my skirt and cross one leg over the other, anything to dull this need for him.

With Roman's hand on the small of my back, he guides us in behind his father.

"You weren't going to visit?" I ask him once we're in the hall.

He shakes his head. "I wasn't, but you gave me new inspiration. I want everyone to meet you and know you're mine."

I can hear the loud chattering of a myriad of voices echoing down the large hall.

"Wow, this place is gorgeous," I say, taking in the vaulted ceilings and intricate stonework pillars.

"Mmmhmm, not as stunning as my wife, especially when she's this worked up."

I slap his bicep. "I have to meet your entire family and I am on the verge of coming while introducing myself to them."

"But you won't. You know what happens when you disobey my orders. Remind me of the rules..."

I pinch the bridge of my nose as my orgasm starts to build. I can feel it in every inch of me, consuming me.

"I only come when you tell me to."

He nods with an approving smile.

"Exactly. Now, be my good girl, introduce yourself and then, maybe, I will let you have what you need."

Relief washes over me as he grabs my hand.

"Oh shit," I hiss as he turns it up a notch. The pulsing hits in a slow, deep pattern that makes my very heart beat feel like it's fucking me from the inside out.

I bite back a grin. This is hot.

Nikolai opens up the double oak doors to the living room. Before I step through, Roman stops me, spins me to face him and slams his lips over mine with his fingers digging into my cheeks.

I do everything I can to fight coming on the spot.

"You don't play fair, Roman," I tell him breathlessly as he pulls back with a mischievous smirk. He shrugs, rolling up the sleeves of his crisp white shirt.

Damn, those veins running down his arms.

As if he reads my mind, he clenches and releases his fist, which almost has me drooling over the way they pop.

"Just a few more minutes, lastochka."

Taking a deep breath, and feeling myself getting wetter by the second, I straighten my spine, take his palm and walk into the lion's den.

A sea of faces turn as we step into the large sitting room. The men all have a familiar look, much like Roman. Hard lines, but kind eyes.

Roman squeezes my hand and ups the vibrations, I can feel them taking over my entire body. I clear my throat to try and distract myself.

Even over all the deep Russian accents, I can hear the toy buzzing, yet no one seems fazed by it.

After they all introduce themselves, I don't know if I'll

be able to remember them. Mikhail is the oldest, and has the friendliest smile when he takes my hand.

Natalia is Nikolai's wife with fiery red hair. She should be easy to remember. Her belly sticks away from her lean frame, and Nikolai can't keep his hands off of her.

Would Roman be like that if I have his baby? He already loves touching me, so I don't think it would be a big leap. The next time we visit, there might be a lot of new children running around, seeing how all of the couples are hanging off of each other.

It's hard to concentrate with the vibrator constantly changing the rhythm deep inside of me. Every time I feel like I'm able to form a word or thought, Roman hits a button making me lose track of what I'm doing.

I can't take much more, so I tug on the sleeve of his shirt. He leans down, taking a sip of vodka, and gives me an innocent look.

"Rom, I'm so close, please help me," I whisper in his ear.

He nods, downing the rest of his drink and slamming it on the counter.

Great, now everyone in the room is looking at me.

"If you'll excuse us, I'm going to give Nadia the famous tour of the house."

The brothers look amongst each other and Mikhail raises a brow at Roman with a grin.

"Father's office is a good place to start."

The flush that spreads up his partner's cheek gives them away.

Nikolai's deep laugh echoes through the hall. "Yes, pay particular attention to the desk."

Natalia's eyes widen, and she lightly pats his arm. "Nikolai," she gasps, turning to bury her cheeks against his broad arm.

I take it Roman's tastes may run in the family.

"Noted."

Roman leads us briskly down the hall, away from the noises of the crowd.

A huge room with an oak desk in the middle.

As the door slams shut behind us, he pins me against the wall, his hand tight around my throat and pushes up my dress.

"I can smell how turned on you are, baby. It's making me wild for you."

He guides my hand to his crotch and a smile as I feel his hard cock pressing against my palm.

"I need you, Roman," I say breathlessly.

"Not as much as I need you," he growls.

I gasp as he slides under my panties and he slowly removes the toy. My eyes go wide when he proceeds to lick it clean and stuff it in his back pocket.

"What does my greedy slut of a wife need from me today?" he asks, pulling my head to the side and begins to suck on my throat.

"D-don't leave marks." His entire family is just down the hall. My words are laced with moans. I can't help it as he slides his fingers inside me, I open my legs wider.

"I'll mark you wherever I see fit." To prove his point, he leans forward and suctions my neck before pulling the skin back with his teeth in a hard nip.

It sends bolts of electricity straight through me.

With a palm around my throat, he swiftly guides us to the desk and bends me over, my hands slam down on the table.

As I open my mouth, he cracks down on my ass and I cry out.

"That was for telling me what to do."

He rubs the sensitive area, kicks open my legs and lines his cock up with my entrance. With both hands on my throat, he tightens his grip as he slams into me, using my neck to push me back against him. He hits so deeply, it's as if I'm being drawn into my own body.

He is all I can feel, over and over as my head gets fuzzier.

"Such a good girl, aren't you?" His voice is hoarse. I can't reply, I don't have the air to do so.

No matter how many times we do it, each time gets better and better. This man knows every inch of me and how to work me up into a frenzy for him.

"So. Fucking. Perfect," he grits out between thrusts and it sends me to the edge.

"Please, Rom." Is all I can manage to beg.

He loosens his grip, enough to allow me to suck in some air.

"Be a good girl and come on my cock, let me feel how much you love me fucking you."

I let the orgasm take over me, the ultimate high and he doesn't let up the pace. He takes every part of my pleasure until he reaches his own point.

With my name coming out of his mouth like a chant, I feel his warm seed spill into me and I slump against the desk, letting my muscles melt.

As he slides himself out carefully, he puts my panties back in position.

"That all stays in there, lastochka. Got it?"

"Hmm, yes."

He places a soft kiss on my shoulder and helps me to stand, tugging down my dress over my ass for me.

His hands frame my face as we stare into eachothers eyes.

"You have my favorite look in your eyes, Nadia."

I blink at him.

"What's that?"

"Love," he replies with a smile.

READY TO MEET THE REST OF THE PETROV FAMILY?

Nikolai and his sons are waiting for you on Amazon...

Nikolai Petrov by M.A. Cobb (OUT NOW)– https://mybook.to/28MaTi

Lev Petrov by Harper-Leigh Rose (OUT NOW) https://mybook.to/LevPetrov

Viktor Petrov by Darcy Embers (OUT NOW) https://mybook.to/ThePetrovFamily-Viktor

Mikhail Petrov by Elle Maldonado (Releasing July 14) https://mybook.to/7Twn

Aleksei Petrov by M.L Hargy (OUT NOW) https://books2read.com/u/bwgjRZ

Have you read Luna's best selling series, Beneath The Mask and Beneath The Secrets?

These are stand-alone, dark mafia romances all set in the same universe. Meet these filthy men now on Amazon and Kindle Unlimited:

Chaos, book one, Jax and Sofia- https://mybook.to/jc04FR

Caged, book two, Nikolai and Mila - https://mybook.to/Fc18uiK

Crave, book three, Alexei and Lara- https://mybook.to/rTb4

Claim, book four, Mikhail - https://mybook.to/rTb4

Beneath The Mask

Distance, book one, Keller and Sienna- https://books2read.com/u/mgPk2X

Detonate, book two, Grayson and Maddie- https://mybook.to/3tlYU

Devoted, book three, Luca and Rosa- https://books2read.com/u/brBoxA

Detained, book four, Frankie and Zara- https://mybook.to/PfoRNy

Beneath The Secrets

Chaos, book one, Jax and Sofia- https://mybook.to/jco4FR

Caged, book two, Nikolai and Mila - https://mybook.to/Fc18uiK

Crave, book three, Alexei and Lara- https://mybook.to/rTb4

Claim, book four, Mikhail - https://mybook.to/rTb4

ABOUT THE AUTHOR

Luna Mason is an Amazon top #12 and international best-selling author. She lives in the UK and if she isn't writing her filthy men, you'll find her with her head in a spicy book.

To be the first to find out her upcoming titles you can subscribe to her newsletter here:

https://dashboard.mailerlite.com/forms/232608/79198959451506438/share

You can join the author's reader group (Luna Mason's Mafia Queens) to get exclusive

teasers, and be the first to know about current projects and release dates.

https://facebook.com/groups/614207510510756/

SOCIAL MEDIA LINKS:

http://www.instagram.com/authorlunamason

https://facebook.com/groups/614207510510756/

https://www.tiktok.com/@authorlunamason?_t=8j38HlkCYmP&_r=1

Printed in Great Britain
by Amazon